Jeanie

Johnny

by

Fatal Urge Carefree Kiss

Jeanie Johnny

All rights reserved

Copyright © 2017 by Fatal Urge Carefree Kiss

ISBN 13: 978-0-646-98085-0

ISBN 10: 0-646-98085-8

All names, characters, incidents, and places, used or described in this book, are a work of fiction, and any resemblance to any actual person, living or dead, event or locale, is purely coincidental.

Cover design, illustrations, interior formatting and editing:

Fatal Urge Carefree Kiss

Jeanie Johnny

"Are we there yet?"

Finding Way Through:

And home they make!

Jeanie Johnny

"Perspective is what you see; point-of-view is what you make of it."

A split today

Dated: 21ˢᵗ July, 2101

Observations can be neutral, but judgments are always coloured, by the previous knowledge and personal views of the observer. Furthermore, there's nothing surprising about ten different observers having ten different perspectives for the same situation, and is quite natural to expect some variation in their assessments of the same. However, as long as the observers are honest in their evaluation, and their appraisals supported by observable facts, there would still be a consistency in their conclusions, or rather judgments. This will be true unless there is some fundamental conflict between the observable facts, or the perspectives.

If the observable facts can support two different conclusions, then both conclusions would be correct, even if in direct contrast with each other. Yet there may be a situation where only one conclusion would be allowable to prevail. Which one should, will ultimately depend on the conscience of the situation at hand, and of course, the conscience of the one making the call!

Nothing would illustrate this beautiful yet intriguing conflict better than the very innocent beginnings of this story that started with a child that was barely one, and another that was then yet to be born.

"Man, time sure flies," the gracious lady replied to her friend at the other end of the video chat, "I can't believe this day has finally arrived. Where is Malvin though?"

"He's just fixing Johnny's favourite baby formula," her friend replied, "Oh here he is?" He turned around to kiss his partner Malvin, who had just walked in from the kitchen with his biological son Johnny in his lap, and a bowl of baby formula precariously held between the thumb and fingers of one hand.

"Hi Sweena," Malvin greeted the lady at the other end before turning to his son and planting a kiss on the soft cheek of the bubbly baby, "Hey little Johnny, say hi to Sweena!" He then put the bowl on the table and grabbed Johnny's little hand in his own, to wave at the camera, "Say hi to Sweena."

"Hi Johnny, my cute little bundle of amazing," Sweena jubilantly waved back before a sad expression tinged her look, "Why did time had to fly?"

"I know," Malvin replied as his partner took the child in his lap, "It's a shame that in a few hours time Johnny would be officially one, and then we won't be allowed to organize any more meet ups between the two of you. It's really sad, but I guess there is no other way around."

"Absolutely Malvin," Sweena replied as she held back her tears, "I may have had him inside my body for nine months, but there's absolutely nothing else that I and Juliandra want, but you and Josha to be proud and happy parents of your son."

"Thanks Sweena," Josha replied as he gently rocked little Johnny in his lap, "The child must never know who its' one biological parent is, which is a shame, but perhaps necessary, to enable better integration of men in our society, and women in yours." He then paused before asking, "By the way, where is Juliandra?"

"She's right there," Sweena replied pointing behind herself, before motioning the camera towards her bed, "She is feeling a bit low on energy today. You know; two more weeks and Jeanie will be with us!"

"Jeanie," a happily surprised Josha quipped, "That's a sweet name for the girl."

"Hi Johnny," Juliandra exclaimed from the bed as she pulled herself up into a seated position, "Ouch! She kicked me again." And laughter burst out at both ends of the video link!

"We actually thought Jeanie would be a cool name for our daughter," Sweena replied, "It not only sits sweet on the tongue, but it just rhymes so beautifully with Johnny."

"Oh we sure agree," Malvin replied, "And we are actually kind of glad that it was Josha's sample that helped you with Jeanie." He then looked at Josha to add something.

"Yeah," Josha replied nodding his head, "It just makes us an even closer knit big-family."

"Indeed it does," Juliandra replied and then added the lament, "One that can't even sit together after one year."

"That of course is the downside," Malvin replied, "But hey, you can always see pictures and videos of Johnny every day on my and Joshua's public profile at 'Trouble-makers' social media page. Besides, I will be posting you videos and pictures regularly every month."

"And we will do the same with Jeanie," Sweena replied, "Just because our kids can't know who their biological parents are, doesn't mean we can't share their pictures with each other, hey!"

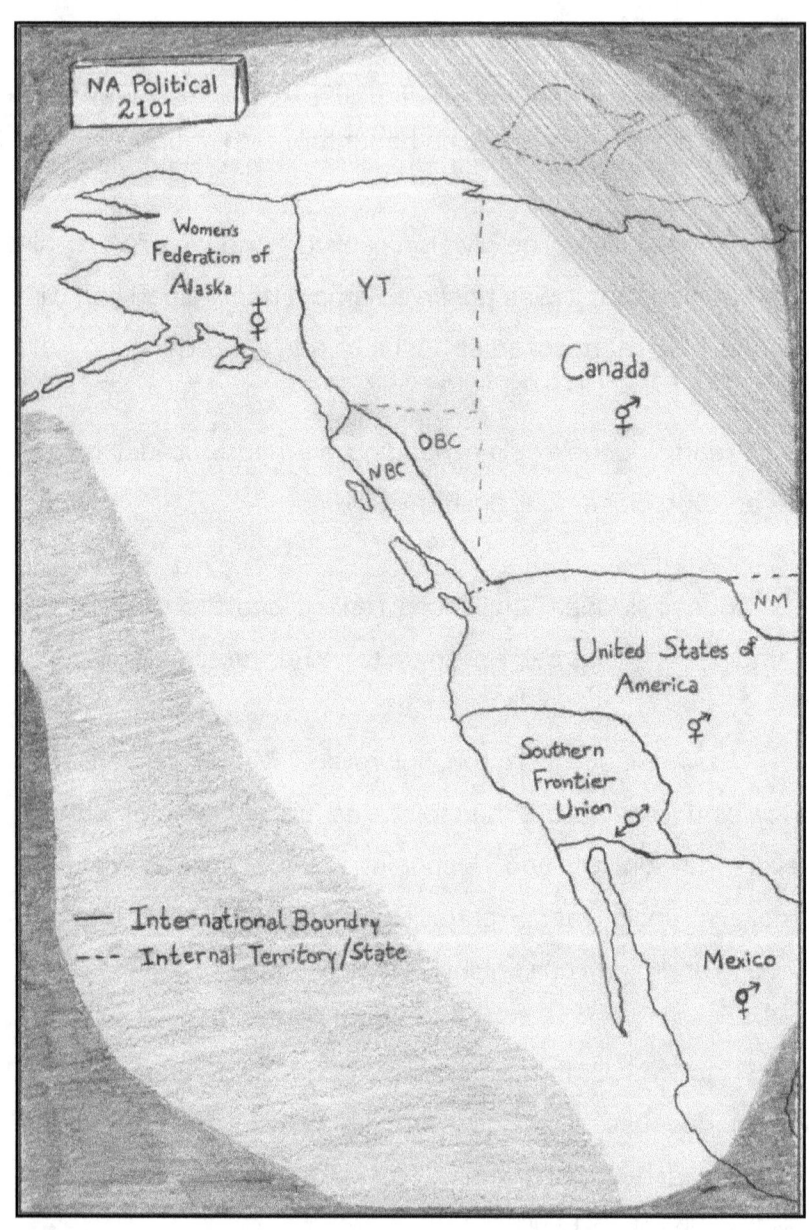

"Absolutely," Josha emphatically replied as he planted a kiss on his son's cheek.

"By the way, how's weather in 'Women's Federation of Alaska' these days?" Malvin asked to turn the conversation.

"The same old freaking cold," Juliandra replied, "You guys are lucky living down there in the beautifully pleasant 'Southern Frontier Union', where weather is always warm and beaches full of life."

"Don't be fooled by impressions Julia. I and Josha are always discussing how beautiful it would be to live in a snow laden paradise!" Malvin replied, before turning around to look at little Johnny, "I am sure Johnny would love to visit it one day."

Jeanie Johnny

"Innocence is spontaneous and emphatic in disputing allegations."

Chapter One: The odd ones out

Dated: 5ᵗʰ August, 2118

Mud doesn't soil a name merely by being flung at it, unless the glue of guilt already smears the plate. The oil of innocence however leaves the plate ready to be wiped clean in one swipe. Men and women, none are above the lies they speak and venom they spew, more when motivated by personal desires. A society can never be morally upright enough, to be rid of moral trash that infests its veins. People will throw allegations at another, if only to bring the other person down. But innocence will always make its way through the moral morass, and guilt be caught in spite of its laborious pretentions otherwise.

Innocence is emphatic and spontaneous in its reaction to allegations, and guilty know this. But hard as the guilty try, to imitate the former, they falter at the very first hurdle; the reasoning that explains away the situation. Now it's true that extravagant circumstances may have affected the actions being questioned, but such circumstances are often an exception rather than a norm in a society. More extravagant the explanations, more convincing the reasoning need be!

Complex as the exposition above appears; the situations seldom rise enough, to warrant a test of analytical faculties of an impartial observer. The conclusions are often foregone, with the only formality left to establish being; when does one accept them. Little did Malvin and Josha know they would themselves be confronted by one!

The three day inter-varsity fair had been a resounding success for another year, with the rookies savouring each and every moment of their new found adulthood. Freedom was in the air, as the last few hours of the festivities gloriously marched towards a late night culmination. The city of 'Los Essence' had come to life with music, games, and companionship overflowing across its' campuses. But like every big city, it too has a dark side to its' vibrant life.

"Do you have any European bands, like the 'Lassies of Glass' or 'Yours Unruly Siestas'," Johnny asked the holobot marketing entertainment licences.

"How about you go buy a pack of latex," an unruly voice however sought his attention, "So we don't feel too hard to you."

Johnny turned around, spite making no mistake in colouring his face, from hairline to chin, "Tell me Shandier, is it really that hard for you to live your own life, and not acknowledge my existence in your gracious kingdom?"

"Your beauty Johnny," Shandier replied as his two mates laid seize around the young man, "It's blindingly

obvious even amongst a crowd." He then raised his hand to try and touch Johnny's face, but Johnny ferociously knocked it away. "Tell me Johnny, are you really trying to save yourself for someone special," asked Shandier sarcastically, before adding, "Or are you queer?"

"None of your business either way," retorted Johnny as he pushed the advancing Shandier back.

"Easy son," one of Shandier's henchmen reminded him that he was surrounded.

"You know very well how we deal with queers here Johnny, don't you?" Shandier continued, "Why make it hard for self? Or are you really looking forward to a masochistic experience?"

"Step away from him bastard," a forceful voice however killed any notions Shandier might have had in mind for the moment.

"If not for Lyaneder, who else would rescue this damsel in distress here," quipped Shandier as he spun around on his feet to face the new arrival at the scene, "Tell me; how long have you been desperate to get his pants down Lyane; since middle school?"

"I bet it was kindergarten," commented one of Shandier's side-kicks as the trio burst out in a self satisfying vile laughter.

"Ask my fist you knuckle heads," however retorted Lyaneder, as he lunged forward to punch Shandier.

But Johnny intervened to stop the scuffle before it had started, "How about you all mind your own business and let me mind mine?" He then pushed Lyaneder back and walked away.

"Listen Johnny," Lyane however tried to catch his attention for a moment.

"You know Lyane," Shandier meanwhile wasn't finished with his taunts, "You may eat his shit out of a plate, and you still won't get a dig." And he walked away with his friends, leaving Lyane there to ponder.

Finally Lyane's temporary trance broke and he rushed behind Johnny, "Hey Johnny, wait. Can I just talk to you for a sec?"

"What Lyane," asked a nonchalant Johnny as he turned around to face Lyane, "What can you say today that you haven't told me so many times already?" His question left Lyane speechless as Lyane came to a halt next to him. "The fair is still not finished Lyane," Johnny advised him like a good man that he was, "Go find yourself someone who can give you as much love, as much you are capable of showering on him." Johnny gave a soft pat to Lyane's shoulder, and walked away.

Who doesn't wish for an opportunity, to walk away from a problem without having to deal with it; wish that someone else would fix it for them? That's the charm of wishes; they help one escape a moment they are physically, intellectually, and psychologically entangled into, even if only for a deceitful second.

"What happened? What did Jeanie do?" a concerned Josha asked Juliandra, as his concerned frame inclined towards the three dimensional videogram.

"They really take domestic violence very seriously here," Juliandra replied, "They are fine with a woman raping another woman, for it helps keep women in line with the state policy. But domestic violence; and it is a straight level three offence."

"She was lucky to escape with a reprimand this time," Sweena added as the camera floated towards her, "But if she beats up her girlfriend again; she's looking at three years in Cryo."

"She is growing up into a very aggressive woman Josh," a concerned Juliandra continued, "She's just turned seventeen today, and already she's raped her girlfriend five times; and boy is she violent! Sometimes I fear she just digs the thought of being a control freak and beyond law, and at others I fear she is just not satisfied with anything!"

"She takes on you," Sweena however had her own axe to grind, "You could be an absolute beast yourself."

"But that's why you love me, don't you?" Juliandra argued back.

"Stop bickering with each other girls," Malvin however interrupted, "You can settle your domestic scores later, but this is important. We over here are really concerned about Johnny?"

"Yeah," Josha backed him up, "We are no different here; rape is legally allowed if any man or boy is deemed queer by his peers. And we are really concerned about Johnny."

"Why?" the concerns of Sweena were instantly raised as well, "Don't tell me he is straight!"

"He's never said so; yet; thankfully," replied a concerned Malvin, "But he is eighteen, and I doubt he's even tested his potential yet, if you know what I mean. The boy has not had a single boyfriend all his life. We are concerned."

"But as much we are concerned," Josha added, "I'd rather have him brought back in line than lose him to a foreign state that we know nothing about."

"Necessary evil boys; necessary evil," quipped Juliandra shaking her head.

"Johnny is here," Malvin and Josha's Soul-of-house announced as Johnny's little car floated across their home's fence.

"Girls, we got to go," Josha quickly replied as he motioned the videogram to log out, just in time as Johnny rushed in. But before Malvin or Josha could utter a word, Johnny's ferocious-set glide-stairs had lifted him up to his room.

"Listen young man," called out Malvin in vain.

Youth is motivated but irrational, aggressive but haphazard, demanding but un-accepting. It knows what it wants, and why it wants, but it seldom understands why not to have it, or if it understands, it rarely accepts not having it. It knows what it has, but will boast of more, disclose less, and acknowledge least. If old age is the most self-preserving phase of life, then youth is the most self-serving.

"We need to talk," Malvin was adamant to settle issues, and thus wasted no time in confronting Johnny in his room.

"About what," Johnny retorted back.

"About you," Josha chimed in to support his partner, "About what you want out of your life; about what you are trying to achieve; and above all; about what you are!"

"And what is that supposed to mean?" Johnny asked.

"You explain it to us son," Malvin replied back, "You are here, back at home well before eight, when tonight you should have been out on the streets partying till late in the morning. And rather than us being worried about you being back home early, we should have been worried about you having not returned at all."

"I just had my share of fun," Johnny, taken aback but calm, replied, "Why is it such an issue?"

"It is an issue Johnny," Josha replied, "And you know why we are asking you these questions."

"Oh C'mon, we are not having this conversation again," and Johnny gave up as he sprung from his bed and threw his hands in air, "I don't know why it bothers you that I haven't hooked up with a guy yet."

"It bothers us because we are your parents," Malvin replied, "It worries us that you are a single at such a ripe age. What is wrong?"

"Why does anything have to be wrong?" Johnny vehemently argued back, "Why can't a guy just take his time in deciding what he wants? What is wrong with you guys? Why are you pushing me so hard?"

"Because you have taken too long," Malvin almost lost his composure, "If nothing is wrong than why are you not like other guys your age?"

"I don't have to be," Johnny's voice too rose in temperature, "I am happy with myself, and I don't need another man to make me happy!"

"Then what do you need; a woman?" this time Josha blew his lid, "Are you queer?" And his eyes dug deep into Johnny's eyes.

Johnny was taken aback, but fumbled back a meek reply, "I don't need to explain myself! It's a personal matter."

"Oh my; you are queer!" Malvin replied as a chilling realization settled deep in his eyes.

"I didn't say that," Johnny protested.

"You didn't deny it too," Malvin quipped as he walked out of his room fuming, while Josha stood motionless behind, staring blankly at Johnny's face.

Jeanie Johnny

"Most potent is the language that speaks through silence."

Chapter Two: Calls from the cot

Dated: 10ᵗʰ August, 2118

Underwhelming is human appreciation of the unspoken word; the word which is felt and not heard. The impact of silence travels beyond the limits of language, for language is confined by meanings. And meanings seldom express anything more than the context in which the content has been uttered, and the mannerism that embellishes it. Silence has the advantage of ambiguity!

But silence is not the only form of unspoken words. Often there are words that run parallel to what is actually being said, but are not required to be spoken themselves. One may label them as the real intentions, desires, or motivation of the orator, but they are nevertheless picked up by the sensitive minds that are alive to the conversation. They are the listener's appreciation of the reality that sits behind what had just been apprised to the listener. They are the untold truth!

Beware are those who care not to hurt feelings, of the words they give their tongues liberty to utter. A sensitive individual cares not just for the words they speak, but also the impact they will have on their audience. But amazing is the contrast that while Johnny is a lot more mature than what his youth might suggest, Jeannie is a total firebrand.

"Hey Max," an excited Johnny exclaimed as he bumped into his old school mate after a long time, "Where have you been my dear friend?" And the bear hug was totally on the menu.

"Great Johnno," Max's glee was no surprise either, for the two nerds had shared a lot more than fierce competition at their school, "Good to see you old pal! What are you studying at the University?"

"Space-law," a proud Johnny exclaimed before asking, "What about you? And above all; where have you been man?"

"Just starting Healthline Commerce bro," Max replied, "Went for a holiday with my partner Tairon, and guess what; we are going to have a baby!"

"What!" a shocked Johnny exclaimed, "Wow!" And he looked around totally taken aback by the surprise news burst. "I mean, wow," he carried on, "I am so happy for you guys!" He shook Max's hand vigorously as genuine happiness took a hold of him, "Boy, you guys sure are quick! Give me all the dirt; now!"

"Well, we just went on a holiday to the US," Max replied, "And before we even finished the adventure, we realized we are in it for the long haul, and then one thing lead to another."

"So, are you going to go the Alaska way too?" a pleased Johnny asked.

"Nothing can replace a real woman's womb bro," Max replied, "We want the best for our child, and nothing beats Mother Nature even in the age of 'Speed-wombs'."

"True that, true that," Johnny quipped shaking his head as he looked down, as if momentarily his thoughts had wondered somewhere else.

"Still thinking about who your mother was, are you?" Max however knew what infested the brain of his childhood companion, competitor and friend.

"Well," Johnny exclaimed, "Not that it really matters, but if only!"

"So your parents haven't told you yet," Max commented as he tried to look into Johnny's eyes for an answer.

"I don't even ask them anymore," Johnny replied, "Lest I hurt their feelings; something I dare not even in my dreams."

"Then you only have one other way left bro," Max replied, "Hook up with a partner, apply for an Alaskan incubator, get there and get the info."

"Can you do that?" a surprised Johnny asked.

"Of course dude," Max replied, "You won't get the name and address, but they will give you the initials of your birthing mother, and the liaising hospital. Something's better than nothing!"

"Yeah, but where do I get a partner just to apply for a child, and then what will I do with the child," Johnny however lamented.

"That is your homework bro," Max quipped, and then patting his shoulder sought his leave, "I better leave now! I'm late for my lecture already. See you later!"

Desire is a guide; not moral, but motivational. It guides one through the maze of problems, to arrive at the solution sought. The solution however is satisfying only if it is morally perfect. Imperfect morality seldom yields a satisfying achievement.

"Who is my father though?" Jeanie innocently asked Juliandra and Sweena.

"Why do you ask?" Sweena, who was taken aback by the sudden query, asked.

"Just wondering," Jeanie replied with a shrug.

"Why," a thoroughly concerned Sweena however implored her further, "Do you think we don't love you enough?"

"Oh no, you got it all wrong," Jeanie was immediately on the defensive, "I could never ever even dream of such a thing. I love you more than my life, and I know you two love me much more. It just slipped out of my mouth; curiosity!"

"Things like that don't slip out of someone's mouth unless they really want an answer," Juliandra however commented, "But the question is, why would you want to know about someone that you have never met, and probably someone who doesn't even know that you exist?"

"I swear I don't care," Jeanie knew she had unintentionally hurt her mothers', and was genuinely remorseful. However, her desire to know wasn't really all that unintentional, for she still let a query slip out of her mouth, "I just was curious if it was a man or just a sperm."

"Why should it bother you today, after all these years," Sweena complained, a bit agitated now, "We know you love us more than anything, and you know that we love you as much, but then; why would you want to know if someone else was involved in our lives? Why are you not satisfied?"

"Guys, you are taking it too seriously," Jeanie finally protested, "It was just an innocent query!"

"For you it might be an innocent query," Juliandra however argued back, "But for two mothers who have left no stone unturned to give their piece of heart the best in the world they can manage; it is a spade through the heart!"

"Look, I'm sorry," and Jeanie broke down, "I didn't mean to hurt you in any way. It's just that I was curious to know who else could be a part of my life; the source of it."

"Why should anyone else, that too a man, be a part of your life Jeanie?" an even more concerned Sweena asked her.

"Because I have a right to know who my father is," finally Jeanie let her angst out, "Not because I want him in my life, but just because I deserve to know."

"And which one of us would you want to get rid off should we tell you that," an even more ferocious Juliandra shouted back in her face, silencing her for good. The duo wasted not a moment and walked straight out of Jeanie's room, leaving Jeanie to ponder over what had just transpired.

Life can sometimes outpace you, and sometimes you may rush ahead of it. As long as you are following what you need to do, or doing nothing at all, life is ahead of you. The moment you start doing today what will yield results tomorrow, you jump ahead of it. Wise are those who follow life by doing things needed to be done today, which nevertheless will yield results in an unknown future too. It's like raising a hen for eggs until one cooks it when it won't lay no more.

"You have a guest," Max's Soul-of-house intimated him the arrival of a long time friend.

"Let him in," Max exclaimed as the door opened for Johnny. "Johnno," exclaimed an exuberant Max, as he rushed ahead to hug his equally happy pal.

"Listen, I've come to you for only you may be able to help me on this one," Johnny exclaimed without wasting a moment in formalities. There was place for none between the two old time pals.

"Say it my friend, and I'll turn the world upside down," Max exclaimed, "At least as much as I can shovel without tiring."

The two laughed, but Johnny was quickly on with the business pestering him, "Listen Max, about what you told me today afternoon; I need help finding a guy who would assist me as a partner."

"You are not serious," a concerned Max however exclaimed, "You are not going to fake a relationship just to know few inconsequential bits about your mother." The resolve on Johnny's face however had him shaken, "By damn, you are serious!"

"That's the only way to know at least something about my mother Max," Johnny argued in support of his suggestion, "You know how much it means to me."

"It's not just about you Johnno," Max however wasn't impressed with his friend for the first time in his life, and thus vehemently argued, "There is going to be a child involved. What about that child?"

"There won't be," Johnny's calm and composed response however surprised him.

"I don't get it," Max was expectedly surprised, "How will you get to the 'Women's Federation of Alaska', without an intention to hire a womb?"

"Simple! I will let the authorities know I have changed my mind once I've got the information that I need," Johnny however thought he had everything figured out.

"They will kick you out before that," Max countered his suggestion, "You can't just walk in there, get information and get out. You will need a local guarantor, and none other than the woman who would lease her womb. And even she can't help you until you have a confirmed implantation. Read the rules of maternity 'Space Lawyer'."

"Don't worry about that," Johnny however appeared to have figured out a solution already, "I'll get her abort the pregnancy before it is too late. She'll get the money, I'll get the information, and everybody will be happy. Simple!"

And Max was left staring at his friend's face.

Jeanie Johnny

"One expects more from friends than what one might do for own beloved."

Chapter Three: Got your back

Dated: 14ᵗʰ August, 2118

L ove is draining while friendships are demanding. Love drains the one afflicted emotionally, physically, and financially. And love drains not because the beloved's demands are overbearing, but rather because the lover is keen to give, and give more than what the lover can actually afford to give. Love is an unequal relationship; the beloved is always at a pedestal, while the lover is always a plea maker, an appeaser. The power differential of this relationship is second to none, not even to that between a god and a believer. The beloved never even need make a demand, for everything is forthcoming without a call.

Friendships however are equalizing, even when not between equals. And by its very nature; equality demands a balance across the two sides. Friends don't need to appease each other, but friends expect friends to answer their needs should a situation arise. If a friend has to ask for a favour, than the friendship never really existed, else the other would have already pre-empted the request by offering unconditional help. But unlike love, this is still an offer, not a unilateral gift. Friendships don't drain, but rather multiply, the joys, comforts, and peace. Friendships are about self satisfaction, that you did your friends right. But of course, friendships are also about expectations that one's friends would do for them, at least as much as they are themselves ready to do. And what one thinks they are ready to do for their friends does not have to be the same as what they actually offer to do. It is just a hypothetical yardstick to judge what to expect from your friends; a yardstick worse than arbitrary.

Of course, there is love in friendships, and friendship in love. But the overwhelming chemistries of the two relationships are still unadulterated by these involuntary infusions. This is why raising kids is draining, while growing up as siblings is satisfying yet demanding. Both Juliandra and Sweena can vouch for it; or at least one half of the statement.

"Mom, can I talk to you two for a sec," Jeanie sought her two mothers' attention.

"If it is about that Mars trip that you have been harping about lately, then you already know where we stand on it," Juliandra however was firm on the stand she and Sweena had taken.

"But mom, I swear I'll pay every cent back to you before the end of next winter," Jeanie pleaded, "It's a bumper deal and includes a five night stay at the famed 'Moon Safari Resort'. Mom, please!"

"If you want to go on that trip, then you need to earn and save for it," Sweena made it clear the two of them were in complete unison on that matter.

"But that would take five years," Jeanie fretted, "I'll be old by then."

"You still won't be hanging in your grave when you make the flight," Juliandra quipped with a smile, "Besides, how were you planning to pay us by next winter?"

And Jeanie knew she had been caught in the web of her own making.

It's a lie that men discovered tools, or rather the art of tool making. Spiders had beaten them to it probably by millennia. One can argue spiders are evil, for they have eight limbs and yet then need to spin a web to trap innocent victims. But is it really their fault that they are meticulous in planning, so they can be lazy in life? After all, isn't that what humanity has strived to achieve for ages?

"Johnny," Lyaneder sought Johnny's attention, even if it meant he had to disturb an entire silent book-beaming area of the library.

"What Lyaneder, I was almost finished with the subject being beamed into my eyes," Johnny wasn't impressed, "It better be something better than what I have come to expect to hear from you."

"Why do you have to judge me even before I have spoken a word?" Lyaneder complained.

"Silence," was the thundering roar of the librarian, and Johnny reluctantly got off his learning portal and motioned Lyaneder to walk outside with him.

"What do you want Lyane," asked Johnny the moment they stepped outside.

"Max, he told me something; that you need help," Lyaneder replied.

"What? That idiot," Johnny exclaimed in frustration, "Look Lyane, I am sorry. It's not that I don't like you as a person. You are a good guy. It's just that I know how you feel about me."

"And how is that a problem for you?" Lyaneder inquired, "I am not here because I want something from you. I only thought maybe I can help you."

"That exactly is the problem Lyane," Johnny explained, "You want to impress upon me that there's nothing in it for you, and yet you know very well this would be a favour I won't be able to repay lightly. It would be a favour that would make me indebted to you forever."

"Why do you have to treat it as a favour?" Lyaneder asked, "Why can't a friend do something for a friend?"

"But we are not friends, and we can't be friends Lyane, and you know that," Johnny argued back, "You have feelings in your heart that I am aware of. And those feelings mean I will never be able to look at our relationship like a friendship."

"Perhaps you are right," Lyaneder too knew Johnny's words carried weight, but he also knew the situation Johnny was in, "But then how are you going to find someone to assist you? You know the position you are in!"

"I do," Johnny replied, "But that doesn't mean I should make a choice that I might regret for the rest of my life."

"What if I don't do it as a favour?" Lyane however had another proposal.

Johnny's curiosity was immediately raised, "What do you have in mind?"

"How about you sponsor my University for the rest of my Bachelors degree?" Lyaneder asked, "That way I won't be doing you a favour, and you will get someone you can trust."

Lyaneder's proposal immediately caught Johnny's attention, for he pondered for a few seconds before nodding his head, "That does seem to be a winning proposal Lyane."

"Good, then let us set the ball in motion tomorrow itself, and then book our trip," Lyaneder wasted no time in setting out his complete plan.

"Our trip," Johnny however was confused, "But you don't need to come with me to WFA."

"Are you silly," Lyaneder quipped, "Why would I miss an opportunity to visit WFA, especially when I won't be the one paying for the trip?" And he smirked at Johnny, who knew the whole thing was going to cost more than a petty penny, and perhaps all his savings for the next three years, but realized he didn't have a better choice.

Choice is a luxury that is not available to everyone all the time. Clichés aside, sometimes what appears to be a choice is merely a mirage, for the decision is already a foregone conclusion for the protagonist involved in the situation.

"Are you crazy?" Katie, Jeanie's girlfriend was outraged by her proposal, and immediately jumped out of the recliner, "Why would I want to rent my womb?"

"Because I want to get our arses on the Mars shuttle next winter," an overbearing Jeanie breathed down Katie's slowly sinking frame as Jeanie towered over her aggressively.

"But we are not even married yet," Katie protested, albeit a bit weakly.

"Doesn't matter," Jeanie replied as she grabbed Katie's neck in her hand, her thumb nail scratching Katie's face, and her lips lurking close to Katie's lips, with teeth menacing her. She groped Katie with her other hand and pushed her frame back hard into the cushion, and knelt by her side on one knee, while putting her weight on Katie's thighs. "Besides, the kid is not going to stay with you anyway," Jeanie exclaimed as she dug her teeth into Katie's lower lip, making the poor lassie squirm and whine.

"But why don't you do it yourself," Katie feebly asked once Jeanie left her lips to let her breath.

"Because a Mars trip is not a reason good enough for me to ruin my figure bitch," Jeanie replied as she pulled Katie's hair back.

"What about me?" Katie protested.

"What about you bitch?" Jeanie exclaimed as she forced herself on Katie so hard that the recliner overturned. But Jeanie wasn't going to let Katie out of her grasp. She was all hers for the night!

Jeanie Johnny

"Easy rests the head that either carries no debt, or no brain."

Chapter Four: Ruckus raise

Dated: 25ᵗʰ August, 2118

Worry defines the girth of human intellectual prowess. A mind perturbed by the most insignificant of issues is the mind most disturbed, and a mind unmoved by mountains is the mind of a champion. A mind oblivious to worries is the mind of a simpleton, and a mind worried about others' problems is the mind of a saint. Every worry denies rest but seeks solution, and every solution devised leads to intellectual growth. Lasting and strengthening however is the growth that originates from a worry that dwelled upon the worst of problems, and insignificant is the growth that germinates from worries most ludicrous.

Seldom rests the bearer of a mind burdened by debt, and easy rests the one who owns nothing. When worries become fears then wisdom starts the casualty line. Those who are consumed by their fears are consumed so, for their minds stopped spotting exits. Theirs are the minds sandwiched in the middle of a firestorm, and all they see is fire, approaching from every direction. What they miss to notice is the direction the wind is coming from, for heat masks every breeze that grazes their bodies.

Mind is what makes men kings and paupers, and mind is what defines the insane. Mind is where a human's individual identity resides, and mind is where one needs to find peace. Johnny and Jeanie both need to find peace in their minds before their quests consume their sanity, quests they are themselves unaware of, for their minds haven't yet identified what it is they are really seeking.

"There it is, the last piece of information that we needed for arrival clearance," Lyaneder exclaimed as he flicked the message on his holographic display towards Johnny's, as they sat in the University football grounds, planning their trip, "We've finally got the names of the three possible womb providers; Lizzy Turner, Katie Sytsevich and Angelica Boldashevich."

"I am sure one of them would agree to assist me," Johnny exclaimed, "I guess we are ready to fly out tomorrow morning then."

"Can I ask you one thing," Lyaneder exclaimed, "Do we really have to fly out so early in the morning? I mean; we could take one of the evening flights too!"

"Look, we'll get their very early in the morning, have our breakfast at the hotel and then check in and still pay for tomorrow night only," Johnny explained, "And yet we'll have the entire day to ourselves, to check-out the city and the people there."

"City I like, but their people I'm not interested in," Lyaneder replied, "As much as I am sure they won't be interested in us."

"It is not about sexual interests Lyane," Johnny knew what Lyaneder was hinting at; "It is about whether the women there are friendly and welcoming like our people."

"And why won't anyone be warm and welcoming towards tourists?" Lyaneder however wondered, before turning the topic, "Anyway, if we are flying out so early, then you make sure you get to my house at least fifteen minutes prior to your intended departure time for the airport."

"But the airport is closer from my place," Johnny however wondered, "You should be coming to my place instead."

"I know, but Jack fails to get me up every time," Lyaneder explained, referring to his Soul-of-House, "That AI software is not designed to pester people, you know. It works on the willingness of the people to co-operate and order, rather than be a persistent irritant, which is exactly what is needed to get me out of bed every morning. You don't want to find out right on time that I am still not up."

"You pull that stunt on me, and I'll leave you here," Johnny however wasn't impressed, "I've never been to your place, and you are not driving me out that way when I don't have to."

"Oh c'mon man, why make such a big deal about such minor things," Lyaneder exclaimed, "Ok fine, just give me a call in the morning, and make sure I get out of my bed, and I'll come to your place."

"That's alright," Johnny exclaimed, "I'll come and pick you up. But be ready."

"Cheers buddy, I knew you won't let me down," Lyaneder got carried away and tried to hug Johnny, who pushed him back. Avoiding awkwardness Lyaneder asked, "Have you told your fathers about it?"

Selective information is always misinformation, and seldom helpful. It is designed to assuage the one who needs to be worried. But then, it is the trust of the one who needs to be worried, that sells them that information in the first place.

"We are so happy for Johnny," a delighted Sweena exclaimed, "How's the man he's found?"

"Lyaneder is a good boy," Josha, the proud father, replied, "We've known him since Johnny's middle school. He was always in love with Johnny."

"Yeah, we are hoping their upcoming US trip will cement their relationship for the long haul," Malvin chimed in, "By the way, how is Jeanie doing with her girl, what's her name; Katie?"

It is easy to lose the essence, meaning, quality, and importance of freedom, especially when right to being aware is degraded to the right to being a party. Freedom is not important because it gives one the right to live their life on their own terms. Freedom is important because it give one the right to question others when everybody else's quality of life gets eroded.

"We 'Brazen Babes' have a lot of respect for you here Jeanie," the highly tattooed babe quipped as she handed the wheel of Jeanie's car back to her, "We'll love to have you as a Brazen Babe."

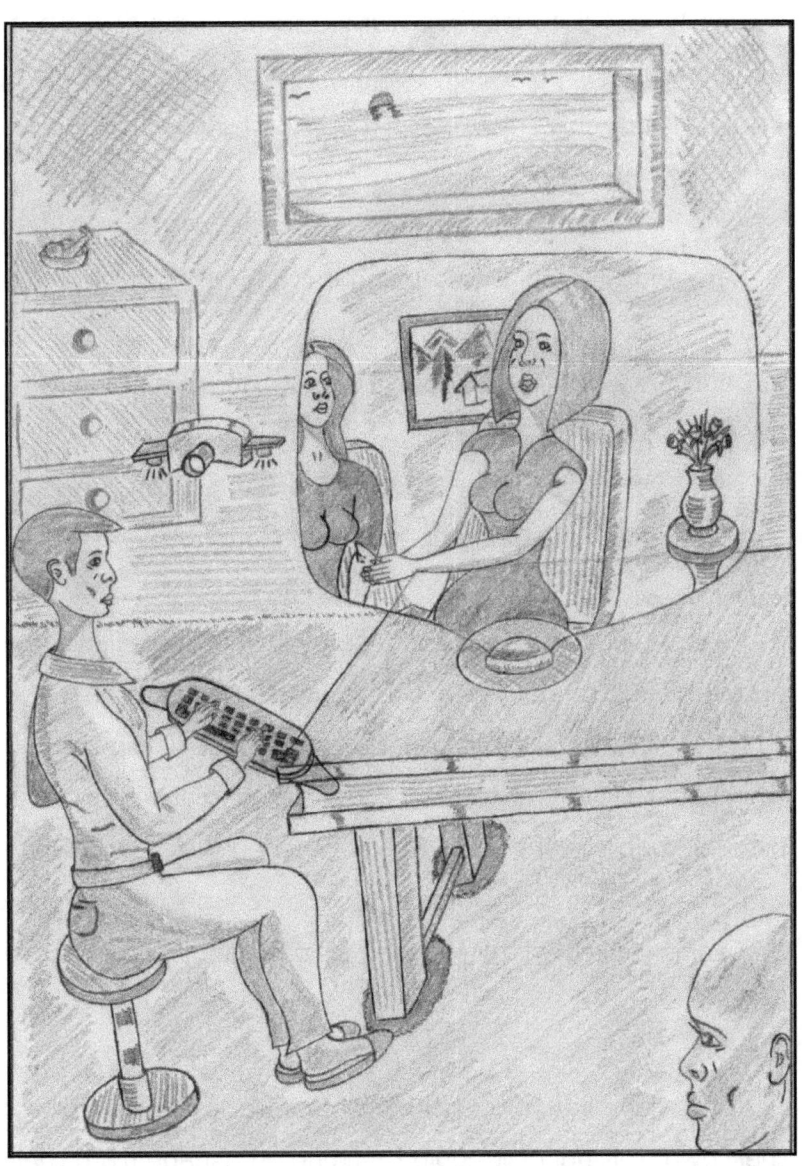

"I know Crystal," Jeanie replied with a nod of appreciation, "It's just that I am averse to every form of authority or discipline. And being a part of a gang as strong as BB, requires a hell lot of discipline, and would involve authority."

Her words had Crystal and her gang in splits, "You know girl, that's exactly why we love you. No bloody respect for authority at all! You are going to do something real-nasty-big one of these days."

"I hope so," and Jeanie joined in the laughter.

"By the way, we have bypassed your car's tracking and auto-pilot controls," Crystal however had things to describe to her, "Here, you see that little switch just below the joy-wheel; just flick it up to take absolute control with no one breathing down your neck. But be warned; flick it only when you absolutely need it, for if you get caught, it is a fifty thousand ticket with license disqualification for three years."

When one cannot distance themselves from the acts of their own making, how could there be an escape from their liability? Yet people end up forfeiting better thought in worst times when they have the least self-control. Hormones exert better influence on human actions than conscious brain.

"I'm sorry dude, I'm so sorry," a very repentant Lyaneder exclaimed as he found Johnny breathing down his neck at four in the morning, "I swear, just give me fifteen minutes. Just come in!"

"Dude, I really hoped this won't happen," a whining Johnny exclaimed before asking, "What about this cab?"

"We'll catch another one," Lyaneder exclaimed, "Just give me fifteen minutes."

"You man," Johnny shook his head as he picked his baggage out of the cab and let it go, "You take one minute more than fifteen and I'll leave you behind."

"Cheers buddy," a pleased Lyaneder exclaimed, "Trust me, I take very little time getting ready." He then escorted Johnny into his living room, but before Johnny could take a seat he continued, "You know I just bought some Euro pop licenses last night, and boy is that the stuff you would like to listen to!"

"Really," Johnny exclaimed in excitement, "What bands did you get?"

"It's literally the best of Euro-pop; 'Lassies of Glass', 'Yours Unruly Siestas', they are all there," Lyaneder exclaimed, "You want to check them out while I get ready?"

Johnny thought for a few moments before agreeing to the idea, "Might as well!"

"Sorry but you'll have to hook up to my system in my room, for I haven't transferred licenses to the house system yet," Lyaneder replied, leaving Johnny in a bit of a spot, "Feel free man, I won't take too long."

"Ok, fine," a reluctant Johnny agreed as he left his baggage and personal device behind and followed Lyaneder upstairs to his room.

"Get him," was a sneaky cry that originated from behind the inside wall as soon as Johnny stepped in behind Lyaneder. In a flash Shandier and two of his mates had grabbed a hold of Johnny from his arms and torso, while Lyaneder turned around and quickly grabbed his legs. The newly formed gang of four lifted a struggling Johnny and pinned him face down on Lyaneder's bed.

"What the heck are you doing Lyaneder," Johnny protested strongly.

"Teaching you how to be a subdued wife bitch," Lyaneder quipped as Shandier and his sidekicks burst out in vile laughter, "Hold him fast while I get my pants down, will you?"

But as soon as Lyaneder let go Johnny's legs, Johnny pulled his arms hard towards himself while Shandier's mates tried to pull them out. In a flash Johnny kicked up hard and into Lyaneder's groin, making him cry out in pain and roll into a ball on the floor. Then Johnny, rather than pushing his arms towards himself, flung them out, making the duo holding his arms lose their balance. Then the black belt in Judo and a black belt in Taekwondo, wasted no time in flinging Shandier off his back and on to the floor. In a flash Johnny was on his feet, and a punch each in their heads, was enough to put the four morons out for the remainder of the morning.

Jeanie Johnny

"Truth is not a spark, but an eternal lamp that can't be left covered forever."

Chapter Five: A mom like you
Dated: 27ᵗʰ August, 2118

Fire cannot exist without a spark igniting it first, and neither can it last beyond its fodder. Allegations are like sparks that light fires of infamy, that last until the last of the minds have been touched by their heat, and those minds have finally dealt with those allegations and moved on. All that fires leave behind as trace are ashes of burnt substrates. All that allegations leave behind are memories; good for none, and bad for some.

Truth however is neither a spark and nor a fire. It is rather an eternal flame; a flame that originates every time a fact comes to birth. It spreads like no fire, and it seldom rises to burn everything. It rather flourishes to light the dark that tries to mask it. Corrupt however attempt to mask the light they can't extinguish, layering it with thick sheets of lies. Eventually the pile collapses and falls on to the flame, to be set alight and start a torch that shines even brighter. The torch burns until every corner of the universe around it has been lit. And once its job is done, all that it leaves behind is learning, but no ash, for lies are vaporous, something that never had a body of substance to burn.

Much tries the liar, to cover their act with niceties of mannerism, yet truth will find a way to shine past their shadows. Lies may work not because they are convincing, but because their victim was temporarily blinded to the truth. But eventually when dark covers all, truth reveals itself. Johnny is in wait of one such revelation.

"So, what do you say," an anxious Johnny asked his hostess, who had been clearly taken aback by his proposal, "Would you assist me?"

"I," Lizzy however struggled to contain her outrage, but maintained her composure lest she be found short in dignified hospitality. After fumbling with words for a few seconds, she decided the best course would be to be loud and clear to Johnny, "Look Johnny, I appreciate you being clearly upfront and honest about your intentions, but unfortunately I and my partner can be no part of your designs. We don't need your money. We were really keen on building an extended family with good people!"

"I am sorry if I have caused you any offence," Johnny tried to pacify his hostesses' rising emotions.

"It is an outrage," finally Lizzy could no longer bear his nonsense and rose out of her seat, "I have heard enough! I and my partner are strong pro-life supporters, and you want us to either ruin a life or end it before it has even exercised a right to exist, only so you could satisfy your pathetic curiosity!"

"Please! Don't get me wrong," Johnny got up from his seat too, his hands gesturing the lady to calm down.

"You are wrong!" Lizzy however roared back, "The least favour that I can do for you is that I won't be the one to notify the authorities, provided you drag your filthy presence out of my house immediately. But I warn you; be very careful with anyone else, for two reversals would bring authorities directly into your future negotiations. Now get out of my house right away."

Waiting any further would have been a catastrophe.

Everyone prepares for bad times, but none expects random catastrophes to destroy their whole lives. It is one thing to prepare for flood and fire, and another to be sucked into a sink-hole. But that is the unpredictability of life; the one that makes people fear the unknown and stay in line. But what really is the line, especially in times of volatile morality?

Jeanie was driving home after finishing another long day at University and work, when an unknown figure suddenly rushed out of a side street and nearly bumped into her car. For someone who loved flying her car in manual mode, Jeanie did well to stop it in time.

"What the hell is your problem bitch?" Jeanie let out a mouthful of profanities as she gestured her window to wind down. But she didn't have to wait for the answer, as a horde of rowdy bike riders emerged out of the street straight away, and came to a stop directly behind the lassie in distress.

"Please help me," the frail and clearly roughed up lady pleaded with Jenny as she made her way around to her side of the vehicle, "They are trying to rape me."

"Look who's here," the leader of the wolf pack exclaimed as she realized who the person in the car was, "Our girl Jeanie." She took off her helmet and continued, "It's us babe, the Brazens."

"Hey Crystal, what's up babe," Jeanie exclaimed as the side door vanished to let her step out of her car, "What are you girls doing here?"

The poor lassie having realized that she had probably run into a person who is on good terms with those she was running away from, tried to make her escape, but this time the Brazen Babes were on top of the situation, and two girls jumped ahead of her to block her exit.

"She's queer," Crystal replied to Jeanie's question, "Wants to immigrate to Canada! But tonight we are going to bring her back in line."

"Oh," Jeanie exclaimed, "So she's your girlfriend."

"Nah, we don't know her," a nonchalant Crystal replied, "Care to join us in fun."

"So you just know her," Jeanie however asked.

"How does it matter?" Crystal replied, "Someone gave us a heads up on this bitch, and we plucked her out of her car after her shift. Now we are going to tuck her in our beds, one by one. We got one spare bed if you care!"

"Let her go," Jeanie however had something else on her mind, and her words certainly eased some nerves on the lassie's face.

"What," Crystal however was shocked.

"I don't mind girls raping their girlfriends to maintain their household," Jeanie replied, "But raping someone you don't know; sorry, can't support that!"

"What difference does that make, and what's it to you anyway," Crystal argued back, a bit offended this time.

"Her existence is of no imperative value to you, and her life of no significance," Jeanie continued, "You don't even need to acknowledge that she breathes the same air that you do. Ignoring her should not be a question of choice, but rather a foregone conclusion."

"And minding your own business should be your mantra bitch," a visibly upset Crystal laid down the rules for Jeanie, "You are beginning to piss me off now. So step aside!"

"I am not standing in your way," Jeanie replied, "And neither is she!" Jeanie grabbed the hand of the poor lassie, and pulled her close to herself. "We are on our way, you take yours," Jeanie exclaimed.

"Is that so?" Crystal quipped with a smirk, "We got two honeys babes! Who's in?"

"Yeah!" roared the gang of five in unison.

"Let's get them then," roared Crystal as she ferociously flew her bike towards the damsels in the middle.

But Jeanie had a lot more than a surprise for her. She jumped in air and kicked Crystal off her bike, and then pulled out a weapon from under her sock as soon as she landed. Two laser hits were enough to knock off the two riders approaching her from behind, while she jumped again to dislodge the remaining two. Before anyone could comprehend what had just happened, Jeanie had her weapon pointed at Crystal's head, "One wrong move and I'll splatter your head across their filthy faces."

The four stopped in their strides.

"Tell them to get out of my sight in five seconds," Jeanie was mean and firm in her words as she bent over, looked deep into Crystals' crystal eyes, and breathed down her neck.

Clearly aware of her precarious position, Crystal nodded to her gang members to get out of there.

Once everybody else had left, Jeanie finally let Crystal leave.

"We aren't finished," Crystal warned her before departing in haste.

"Good, I don't like half baked stuff either," Jeanie quipped before she turned towards the lassie, "What's your name bitch?"

Identity is merely a formal label that distinguishes its bearer from everybody else. Identity is neither the source of one's relationships, and nor a definition of them. Rather it is the love, or lack of it, and the limits imposed on the feelings involved, that identify a person's relationships with others, as well as define them. And love is not a function of conscious thought, but rather subconscious connections.

"You girls wait here and mom would be back before you two would count to one hundred," the lady told her young twins before turning to car's intelligence system, "And you Miss Fenny; keep my kids comfortable."

"As you wish my great lady," Fenny replied in her peculiar tone.

Barely however had the lady stepped inside the boutique, the kids were at their naughtiest best.

"Hey Fenny, how high could you fly?" asked one of the girls.

"Fifty feet and thirty five inches above the ground level," Fenny replied.

"You lie," the other girl teased her.

"Fenny doesn't lie," Fenny replied as a matter of fact.

"Prove it," the first girl dared her as she and her sister slipped into the front seats.

"Sorry, can't do that," Fenny however was not programmed to take such an instruction from the kids.

"Hey fenny what is this lever for," the other girl asked as she pulled up one liver.

"Don't touch my controls," Fenny replied as she tried to override the command from that lever.

"What do these buttons do," asked the other girl as she and her sister went berserk playing with all the buttons and levers in front of them. And then, unfortunately for the two girls, all hell broke loose. The overload of instructions caused a malfunction, or perhaps aggravated an already underlying technical issue, and Fenny lost control of the autopilot mechanism. The car shot off the kerb and headed towards the pedestrian crossing right in front.

"Watch out," Johnny, who happened to be sipping coffee by a kerb side stall, shouted out as he spotted a mature lady trying to cross the road oblivious to the incoming vehicle, lost in the music stream playing in her ears.

"Shit," Johnny knew he had to do something and that too quick, for the car was clearly not in anyone's control. He immediately rushed into the middle of the crossing, made a strong dive, and tackled the lady to the ground, just low enough to escape the car's impact. Luckily Fenny too finally regained control of the car and brought it to a safe stop.

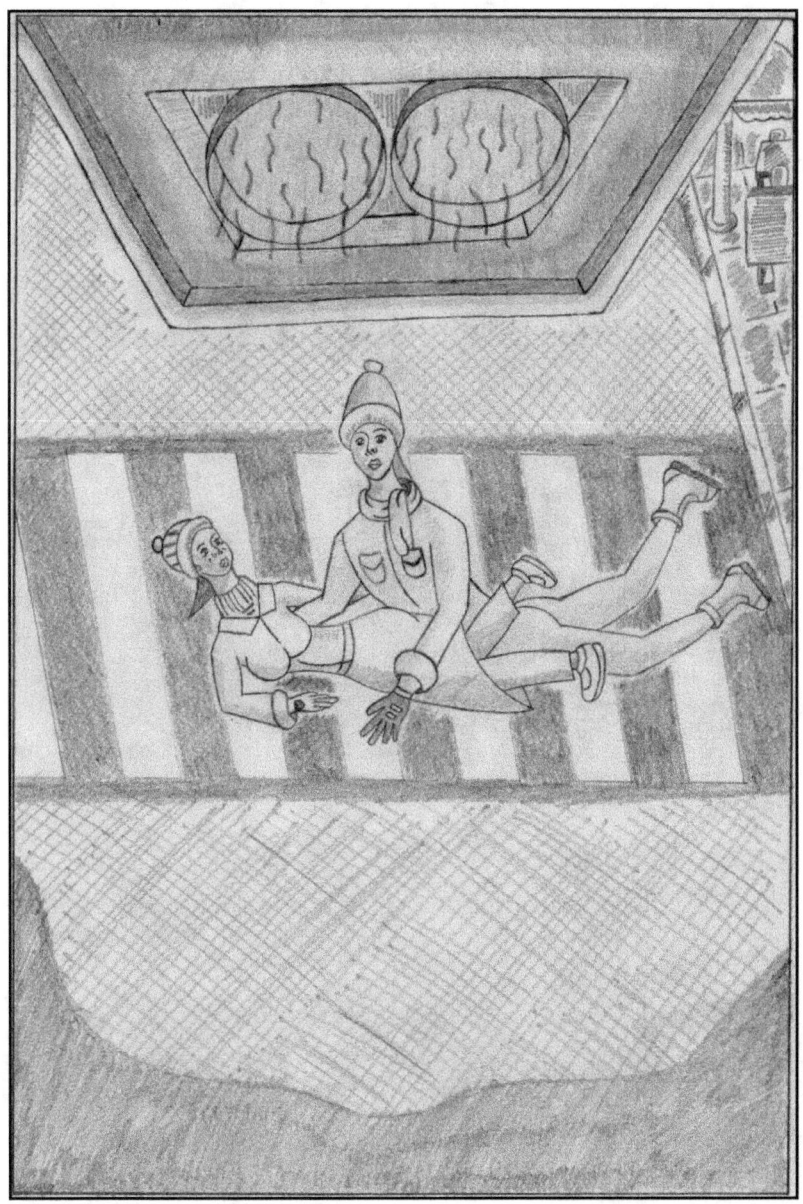

"Are you alright," Johnny asked the lady whose life he had just saved.

"I'm fine, thank you," a surprised Sweena replied as she looked up and realized what had happened, but then her eyes froze on the face of the boy who had just saved her life. It was her boy Johnny, and she was gobsmacked.

"I'm glad you are fine; here take my hand," Johnny exclaimed as he assisted his mother, who he wasn't aware of, up on to her feet. He however found something strangely familiar about her face, and thus asked, "Have we ever met before?"

"Don't think so!" Sweena however replied without hesitation, "I am Lilliane. Who are you?"

"Oh, I'm Johnny," Johnny replied as he shook the lady's hand.

Jeanie Johnny

"A spiritualist simply believes the unknown, while a rationalist seeks to uncover it."

Chapter Six: Tickle my mind

Dated: 28th August, 2118

The question for a believer is not whether a god exists, but rather how to find it. God exists; that is already an accepted truth for the believer. A rationalist on the other hand needs to be assured first if there is any god at all. The starting point of a rationalist's quest lies at the very origins of a stream, rather than somewhere in its middle. What one chooses to believe determines what one would seek further. The direction of actions and their ultimate culmination point is determined by where the starting point is marked on a grid.

Now whatever be the inclination of the one seeking answers, only correct questions yield answers that truly enrich pre-existing knowledge. It however does not imply the one seeking answers would be pleased by the same. When the one asking a question wishes the answer to go a particular way, it is natural for them to not like an answer to the contrary. Yet, the answer invariably has to be sought, for it answers a pestering question once and for all.

Matching questions to already discovered facts is also an art, for matching correct questions will yield thorough understanding. There may be more than one way to question a set of data, and of course, not all ways are right, and not all answers would be correct. Genius is mind that knows how to pick the correct questions without fail. Question however is; are Jeanie and Johnny such capable humans?

"Are you saying you will pay us but you don't want me to have the baby?" a cautious Katie asked Johnny, Then as if seeking Jeanie's approval subconsciously, Katie looked at Jeanie's face and quipped, "I mean that sounds illegal, doesn't it Jeanie?"

"Yes, it does," Jeanie shook her head as she inclined her frame forward on to the table and towards Johnny, "You might have to pay us more!"

"What?" a shocked Katie exclaimed in surprise as her jaw fell to the table.

"You mean you guys, I mean girls, are fine with that," a visibly pleased Johnny asked enthusiastically.

"Of course we are," exclaimed Jeanie, as she put her arm around a bit reluctant Katie, and then let her hand slide down her back, before grabbing a big chunk of her bum cheeks in her grip, and squeezing them hard. Her nails literally dug into poor Katie's skin through her light printed mini skirt, making Katie almost jump out of her seat in pain. "Aren't we sweetheart," Jeanie asked Katie and gave her a fierce look at the same time, "After all, if one human won't help another, who will?" She then turned to Johnny and quipped, "Especially when you are going to pay double."

"What?" this time Johnny's jaw dropped to the table.

"I mean, there's no pressure," Jeanie quipped shaking her head, "You can just leave and talk about it to the next girl or woman, in front of the authorities that would be sitting by your side, since we were your second call."

"That's blackmail," Johnny exclaimed.

"Whatever works dude," Jeanie quipped with a shrug, "It's a mean little world."

And Johnny couldn't hold back his smile, even though his brain knew he had been sucked into it. Smiling he reclined back into his seat, "You know, you are exactly my type of girl."

"What do you mean my type of girl," Jeanie however immediately pounced on his words, her suspicions aroused, and her eyes constricted, "Aren't you the one who's into men?"

"I am technically," Johnny coughed as he corrected himself, "I mean, I haven't just found one yet."

"What do you mean technically, and what about your partner on the profile?" and now Jeanie was absolutely certain there was nothing straight about the person she was talking to, technically.

"Just a friend of mine, helping me out like another human," Johnny quipped, well aware that the girl he was talking to, she may blackmail him to get some more juice out of his pockets, but one who wasn't going to blurt anything out to the authorities, "I just want to know who my mother is, and I was told the only way to know is to hook up with a girl who offers her womb service to you, and then once the pregnancy is confirmed, she can help you get your mother's initials from the record office."

"Oh, just that," Katie exclaimed, relieved as if a heavy burden had been lifted off her chest, "You could have just offered your DNA data to the statistics bureau, and they would have given you the initials of everyone ancestrally linked to you in WFA."

And this time Jeanie's jaw dropped, at the stupidity of her girl. "You moron!' she exclaimed in disbelief, "You just gave him the reason to call off this deal bitch."

"Relax," Johnny however intervened, "The deal's not off, but I think it's time you gave me some discount. I'll pay half of what I originally promised, and your girlfriend doesn't need getting pregnant."

"What, I won't need to get pregnant," and Katie, who had just moved around the table for fear of Jeanie, was delighted at the thought.

"You bitch; we just lost half the deal," Jeanie however rebuked her ferociously, "Now how are we supposed to make up for money lost during the Mars trip?"

"Wait a minute; you girls are going to Mars?" Johnny was curious and interested at the same time, "You know; I've always wanted to go on that trip! How about I join you girls, and we go through Europe?"

"Katie's not going, she's a sissy," Jeanie exclaimed as if totally let down by her girl.

"That's a shame," Johnny exclaimed, "I would have loved to have both of you beautiful girls with me on that trip."

"Are you sure you are into men?" Jeanie was back on to her suspecting best again.

"I told you; I'm not," Johnny added with a naughty laugh, before inclining forward and speaking with intent to pinch, "Why? Are you scared of straight men?"

"Scared of men and me; I come from the school where they don't teach lessons but play 'Lassies of Glass' and 'Yours Unruly Siestas'," Jeanie spoke with an arrogant chiding voice, inclining forward herself, "I'll drink their hearts dry! You better not be one of them!"

"I love and fantasize of them every night before I go to bed," Johnny however calmly replied as he inclined further forward and towards Jeanie.

"Maybe you two should get your DNA matched as well," however Katie, who was clearly not enjoying the quickly warming relations between the two, intervened before things went any further, "You both have a tinge of melanin and who knows?"

"Shut up Katie," Jeanie replied, "He's never ever going to be my brother!"

"I agree," Johnny exclaimed.

There are two ways to face the truth; you face it with your heart, or you face it with your bum. Either way it's going to be a hard smack. The question is; would you rather be dead, or would you rather live to die for failing to pass shit?

"Josh and Mal; where have the two of you been since yesterday," a visibly perturbed Sweena asked as she finally got a video connection with the duo going.

"Sorry we were attending a wedding yesterday in another city," Malvin replied, "Why? What happened?"

"Johnny is here," Sweena replied.

"What? No way," replied a shocked Josha, "He's in the US, holidaying with Max."

"I shook his hand," Sweena went straight for the bulldozer, "And he gave me his name. He saved my damned life from being overrun."

"What?" Malvin exclaimed as he grabbed his head in his hands, "He lied to us?"

"Why is he here?" Juliandra asked; a bit concerned herself.

"We don't know," Malvin replied.

"I think I know," Josha however thought he had a good guess, "He's out there to find which one of you is his mother." He then paused for a quick second before asking, "Sweena, please tell me you didn't tell him anything."

"Of course not," replied Sweena, "I even gave him my wrong name." She then paused as an uncomfortable silence took over their chat. Finally she exclaimed, almost in a whisper, "Although I wish, I could hug him, just once. He was right there in front of my eyes and within my arms grasp; in flesh and blood. And yet I couldn't!"

Wish, wish, and wish; until you either get tired of wishing, or until you actually do something to make the wish a reality. But don't keep wishing until you are too late to do anything about it.

"We do have a match," the girl at the WFA Records Registry replied to Johnny as soon as their lab returned results for his DNA sample, "Your mother's initials are 'S.B.', and she is based in this town only."

"Oh my god, I can't believe this," a shocked Jeanie replied, "That's the same initials as one of my moms."

"Really," Johnny was taken aback by the information, his pleasure of finding the initials of his mother having been suddenly wiped of his face.

"I told you, you two should run a test for yourselves," a rejuvenated Katie added with a big nod.

The duo looked at each other when finally the two exclaimed in unison, "We might as well know the truth right now."

"Great," exclaimed a jubilant Katie, and then she turned around to the girl at the counter, "Could you please run a quick comparison of Johnny's data with Jeanie's data on your record?"

"Sure can," the girl replied, "Although I must say, the system hasn't mentioned any other relations for Johnny here in WFA." But she nevertheless went on to flick a few buttons on the holograph in front of her, and then let it compile the results. "No way," the girl's first couple of words almost sucked the breath out of the duo, but her next words literally gave them a new life, "There's almost negligible, one in a billion chance that you have any relationship, just like any other two absolutely unrelated human beings on this planet."

"You mean we are not related to each other?" an excited Jeanie however wanted to confirm it beyond any confirmation already given.

"No chance madam," the girl replied, "While you are a Caucasian and African mix, Johnny is an Asian and Indian mix. There's no similarity whatsoever in your parentages."

"Did you hear that," an exuberant Jeanie exclaimed as she grabbed a disappointed Katie by her arms, "We are not related." And then she looked at Johnny, who too looked back with a smile beaming across his relieved face.

Jeanie Johnny

"Happy is he who knows someone unhappier than self!"

Chapter Seven: Times a raging

Dated: 30ᵗʰ August, 2118

While love is selfish, care social, and grief vulnerable, happiness is relative. It increases or decreases by the extent of happiness experienced by another. A loss sometimes appears insignificant when a person someone hates or competes with is in a worst situation. A victory can appear insignificant when that other person manages to grab a bigger pie. Such is the hold of jealousy; the best of moments can lose their essence in a moment of hatred.

This unholy alliance of jealousy and happiness reaches the peak of all things sinister, when it's also bound to the selfishness of love. It is easy to be happy and content with someone you love, and it could be intolerably torturous to see one's love happy with another love. One moment one is praying for the well being of their beloved, and the very next they are baying for their blood. Happiness could be sickening in those times!

But when one loves someone, it is hard not to seek the comfort of exclusivity, for it is exclusivity that love itself offers to the beloved. Anything less is dishonest! It is really easy to miss the pointer where love degenerates into possessive control, but it is still all very natural. Katie, the poor battered girl; she still feels her everything breathes in flesh and blood as Jeanie.

It was now the third day of unending indulgence, fun and frolic. Johnny and Jeanie had grown really fond of each other's company, and Katie had been reduced to a mere spare wheel to their joyride. With each passing moment the duo seemed to be getting closer, while Katie was progressively getting impatient. It was like with every joyride taken, every game played, and every sweet cherished, Katie was getting consumed bit by bit too.

"Shot!" exclaimed a jubilant Johnny as Jeanie took out the holographic duck with a blindfolded laser shot.

"Yes!" was the jubilant war cry of Jeanie, as soon as the virtual blindfold vanished off her eyes. The hug was impromptu, and wasn't the first one of the day. Katie however excused herself as the duo turned to invite her for an embrace.

"Your prize," the girl running the blind-shoot game came forward to hand them a lit polygonal box.

"Open it up," exclaimed Johnny as Jeanie tried to force the box open from different ends. "No, no, not like that," Johnny quipped as he took the box from her, "I've handled these before. Let me open it." And then Johnny went about trying his best to open the box until he got frustrated and flung it to the ground, "Shit! Is this thing stubborn?" And he went ahead to try and use brute force himself, making Jeanie burst into a laugh.

"Ha! I thought you were the nerd," Jeanie chided him for opting for brawn.

"It's really consuming to use your brain; I don't like it," Johnny exclaimed.

"Let me help you," Jeanie exclaimed as she knelt down by his side and put her hands on his as the duo squeezed the polygon in its' middle. The polygon finally yielded, but alas their brutality had already dismembered the crystal statue of two horses housed inside it.

"Ouch, that's a shame," Johnny quipped with the raise of a brow before looking at Jeanie, and the two started laughing again.

"I want an ice-cream," Katie however interjected to kill another of their moments.

"Sure, let me get you girls one," Johnny said, "But don't tell me, and let me guess what you girls like."

"Ok, cool!" Jeanie was up for the challenge, "Let me see what you think I like."

"For a strong girl that loves sweet things," Johnny replied, "I am sure you dig the classic vanilla unadulterated."

"Bingo!" exclaimed a surprised Jeanie, and then she turned around to speak to Katie, "He knows me as if he's known me forever." But Katie wasn't impressed.

"Really," Katie tried her best to hide her distaste for their continuing party.

"And you Katie," Johnny said, concentrating hard to guess her taste, "For a girl who loves a dominating person like Jeanie, I think you love the strong taste of chocolate."

"Oh my god, he's totally got it," an even further amazed Jeanie exclaimed as she looked at Katie.

"No, I like strawberry," Katie however replied.

"What are you saying bitch," Jeanie immediately pounced on her, "I buy you a chocolate sundae every time we drive through one of them; the 'Fennaline's Place'."

"My taste has changed," Katie replied as her eyes filled up and she looked straight into Jeanie's eyes.

"Ok fine, I'll get you girls what you want," Johnny exclaimed before walking away to the stall to get their order.

A few minutes later, and walking down the market place inside the theme park, chatting, Jeanie unfortunately dropped her ice-cream.

"Shit," a disappointed Jeanie exclaimed.

"Here, have mine," Katie immediately volunteered.

"Nah!" Jeanie exclaimed, "You enjoy it love."

"You can have mine," Johnny exclaimed, "I like vanilla too." And he offered his half eaten ice-cream to her, and Jeanie grabbed it with a smile.

"Thanks," Jeanie quipped, much to Katie's chagrin.

"You could've taken my ice-cream too," Katie complained.

"I don't like strawberry," Jeanie nonchalantly replied, as she went ahead licking the cone clean.

What one would like is not only determined by their desires alone but, amongst many other things, also by their needs, and means. Morality could also not be underrated in the role it may play when one is about to make a choice.

"Jeanie and Katie have returned with a guest," the Soul-of-house announced as Sweena and Juliandra looked at each other surprised.

"Who the heck it is," Juliandra asked as the duo looked up towards the door.

"Moms," exclaimed an excited Jeanie as she rushed in exulting like a footballer, and then continued on to announce their guest of the evening, "Welcome our friend from 'Southern Frontier Union'." Even before she had spoken the name, a mix of an unknown fear and intense excitement had gripped the hearts of the two ladies, more so Sweena, and the duo rose up on their feet like phoenixes rising from ashes. "Johnny," Jeanie finally let the name drop. And Sweena couldn't help but let her entire body shake as her lungs sucked in a big mass of air.

"Good evening Ladies," Johnny let out the greeting the moment he stepped inside, and was almost half-way through his bow when he noticed a familiar face, "Lilliane, is that really you? I can't believe it." And he rushed forward with an extended hand, as he recognized the face of the lady he had helped dodge death barely three days earlier.

"What did you call her?" a surprised Jeanie however jumped in between the duo, "Her name is Sweena Bazuki, boy."

"What? You must be mistaken! She's Lilliane; I know her," Johnny however insisted, as if he wasn't listening, or perhaps listening but not thinking.

"She's my mom," Jeanie reminded him, with her hands on her waist. And Johnny looked at her, and then at Sweena, and then back at her.

"I'm sorry," Sweena finally joined in the conversation, "I gave you my wrong name. I didn't trust you!"

"That's alright," a stupefied Johnny replied sheepishly, "I guess!"

The duo, Sweena and Juliandra however then made sure they didn't slip on hospitality, and more importantly, made sure they didn't miss a chance to enjoy every moment Sweena's own piece shared with them. Johnny wasn't just bowled over by their affection and hospitality, but he was almost taken aback, in the best sense that could be attached to those words. The evening flew away like it had finally arrived in its jet age.

It is hard to resist stretching out and grabbing what one had sought all their life with passion, when it is right there in front of them for the taking. It takes more than a will of steel and morality of light, for one to stop the horses of their desires in their stead. But should someone dare try and grab the same thing right in front of their eyes; then probably even Hell won't have the fury that one may find their selves capable of unleashing on the disrespectful.

"Wow, doesn't the moon look beautiful tonight," Jeanie exclaimed as she lay on the roof with Johnny.

"Beyond beautiful," exclaimed Johnny, lost somewhere else, as he rested his head on his palm, looking at Jeanie.

Jeanie turned around and saw Johnny gazing intently at her. Their eyes met, and suddenly the moonlight dressing up the roof attained a whole new meaning. "What are you looking at," Jeanie asked as her breathing became heavy, an unknown force grabbing hard her lungs.

"You are so beautiful," Johnny exclaimed. And then their hormones took hold of them, and the two young birds grabbed each other in a passionate embrace, their lips locked as if these were the last few moments left of earth.

Their passions kept rising with each ticking moment as they got entangled into each other. The voice that finally interrupted them sounded much hoarse and worse than what it perhaps actually was, "What the hell are you doing with my girl you freak?" An enraged Katie rushed out of the rooftop opening and lunged at Johnny, hitting him with all her might, "How dare you touch her?" She finally grabbed his hair and literally tore open his skull as Johnny cried out in pain.

"Let him go," Jeanie however grabbed Katie from behind and tried to pull her off Johnny.

"Let go of me," Katie however struggled to try and hold on to Johnny.

But finally the combined forces of Jeanie and Johnny managed to fend her off for the moment. However Katie wasn't the one going to give up. She immediately escaped Jeanie's grip and lunged towards the rooftop opening, yelling in to the Soul-of-house, "Call the damn cops right now!"

Jeanie Johnny

"Truth is really an evil without a cause."

Chapter Eight: Truth hurts; either way

Dated: 30ᵗʰ-31ˢᵗ August, 2118

All it causes is misery; the truth that reveals itself. Blessed are those who remain ignorant forever, for they get to believe what is comfortable. Even those who feel hurt or let down by lies; their pains don't ease by revelations, but only get exacerbated by the knowledge that their suffering was undeserved. It lays waste the alterations put in place by the victims of lies. Above all, it lets down the liars that were counting on its' obscurity. Truth is the trouble maker, for it forces confrontation when everything had already settled, albeit in favour of the wrong side. After all, setting things straight doesn't come without a price itself.

And yet for reason to prevail, truth has to come out; else the fundamental structures of a society would collapse! Lies are like birch shoots growing out of cracks in a wall; the more they grow, the more the wall crumbles. Uncontrolled, they can bring down the entire house. Same goes for society; if every lie succeeds, more people will lie, and suddenly there would be no trustworthy stability in the society. The weight of the elephant would bring it down! Truth has to prevail so the society may continue to exist.

Of course it is equally possible, that if everybody were to start lying, and lies started working; then the society could adapt to it, and work as well as any honest society, albeit in a contrasting fashion. People would know what everything means even though everything would have been stated otherwise. But even then it would be the true meaning that would be running that society, and not the lies that make up the presentations. Sweena, Juliandra, Malvin, and Josha;

they hid the truth from Johnny and Jeanie as long as they could, but now the assumed facts, or rather assumed truths, have created a situation where truth will somehow have to come out and prevail. But what truth would it be?

"I don't understand," Johnny protested, "We are two grown up individuals who have a right to decide what we want to do with our lives." But a hard resounding slap from Sweena silenced him.

The 'all metal and bytes' guardians arrived within five minutes, to formally arrest and lay charges against Johnny; of trespass, assault, and attempting to outrage the modesty of a citizen. Not a word however did Sweena or Juliandra utter, and neither did Johnny ask anything anymore. Jeanie however was expectedly belligerent and immediately set off to arrange legal assistance, for someone who had suddenly become closer to her heart than Katie or family.

Time is always of essence, but more so when life changing decisions are to be made. Things change rapidly in such emotionally intense situations because, on one hand personal desires could be tugging the heart strings in one direction, life liabilities and moral obligations could be tugging them in various other directions. Balance in such circumstances is centred on a very volatile fulcrum.

"What are you doing here in the first place?" an incensed Malvin shouted in Johnny's face, having flown in with Josha on a midnight flight, and having been forced to join the issue with two enraged teens inside a detention room.

"And why should he not be?" Jeanie replied on Johnny's behalf, still belligerent, and still confronting. She may have managed to get all the charges against Johnny declared unsustainable on account of her favourable testimony, but she couldn't stop Katie for alleging lack of proper intentions behind Johnny's visit.

"It's none of your business," Josha shouted back at Katie, "You have no right to speak in our family."

"I give her the right to speak in my support," Johnny too was beginning to feel agitated now, "And I had the right to know who my birth giving mother was."

"And what does that change now?" Malvin shouted back, "Which one of us do you want to stop calling your father?"

"That is not the issue; that was never the issue," Johnny yelled back, "I just wanted to know my entire family, and that includes the one that gave me birth. That in no way meant I wanted to change anything. That it no way means anything has to change between us, and least of all, that we all can't be a bigger family?"

"We are a family already," Sweena finally broke her silence, to silence the young blood once and for all, "I am the mother you came out here searching." And then quickly turning her head towards Jeanie, and raising her voice as if to drive home the point, she finished, "And Jeanie is your sister."

Her words left the two young bloods dumbfounded.

"What?" Johnny finally managed to fumble one word to break the suffocating silence.

"You heard her loud and clear," Josha came out in strong support of Sweena, "And Jeanie was born as a part of me and Juliandra."

And another bout of silence ensued as Jeanie finally realized what the men inside the room really meant to her, more so one of them.

"Do you now realize what it means?" Josha asked Johnny and Jeanie, "We are the same family, and you two are brother and sister!"

Their words were harsh, and represented truth in a way, but not a way that was beyond questions and arguments.

Finally Jeanie rose up from her seat and shouted out hoarse, "He's not my brother! We do not have a single common parent."

"Oh yes he is," Sweena replied with her palm banging down hard on the table in front, "I gave him birth, while my life-partner Juliandra gave you birth, making you too step-siblings. And you can look at this from Malvin and Josha's perspective, and you would still arrive at the same conclusion."

"You cannot mix artificial relationships with natural relationships to serve your own interests," was Jeanie's terse reply as Johnny just watched, still speechless. "You and Malvin are Johnny's parents, while momma Juliandra and papa Josha are my parents. There is no blood-line link between any of you. We two are from two different blood-lines, totally unrelated."

"The relationships that you call artificial today are the very same relationships that you have identified all your life," Juliandra tried to put things into perspective.

"The relationship that I have identified all my life; that of my parents; has nothing to do with Johnny," Jeanie however had an apt reply, "And the relationship that Johnny has identified all his life, has nothing to do with me."

"You cannot deny the link between me and you, and that between Sweena and Johnny," Josha reasoned against her point.

"Just like you cannot create an artificial link between me and Johnny, when it does not exist naturally," Jeanie argued back, "You cannot determine relationships based on your convenience and your desires."

"Argue this back to the society whose norms you dare question," Sweena roared back as Juliandra rose up to grab a hold of her, to give her support as she literally shook with rage.

"Then we will move to a society with better norms," Jeanie replied back.

"Every society is the same," Juliandra too joined Sweena in arguing against Jeanie.

"Not every society," Jeanie however wasn't ready to quit, "The norm that is being ascribed to this society in current situation, is contrary to nature. There are societies where relationships are determined by their natural link, and not arbitrary human choices."

"Enough you stupid girl," yelled Juliandra as her hand rose to discipline her.

"Yes, go ahead and hit me," Jeanie fiercely retorted as she stepped up to face her mom, "But I will speak the truth."

"What you speak is no truth," Juliandra roared back, "It is merely self serving reasoning. It is immoral!"

"It will not become immoral simply by application of an artificial yardstick that is not backed by natural facts," Jeanie retorted back, "And it's no more self serving than you deciding what truth to tell us, when and how to speak it." Her words enraged the four parents in the room even further, but she continued, "You want to create a relationship between me and Johnny that does not exist in nature, while you conveniently denied me and Johnny the knowledge of the relationships that actually existed in nature for us."

"When you live in a society you have to live within its norms and follow its' lifestyles," Malvin tried to argue in support of Sweena and Juliandra.

"Or, we can change the society that we live in," Jeanie argued back, "Which we both have a right to!" She then stepped close to Johnny, and put her head to her bosom,

"We will move to a society where we won't have to suffer a relationship that doesn't exist between us, but rather where we can have a relationship that we truly want to establish between us."

"And that would be no less artificial than those relationships that you have classified as artificial right here," Josha argued back, "You cannot dress immorality in white and claim it to be moral."

"We don't need to dress anything to give it any appearance," Jeanie answered, "What I talk about is a social contract under a society's norms, just like the social contracts that bind your relationships under your societies' contracts. The only difference would be; our relationship would not impose artificial bounds on our kids, like the ones you have imposed on us all our lives, and are still trying to impose anew on us."

"That's it," Sweena was now fed up of this never ending conversation that wasn't going anywhere, "We don't need to listen to any of your rubbish." She then looked at Malvin and Josha, and exclaimed, "You take Johnny back with you on the next available flight, and set him straight whichever way it takes." She then turned to Juliandra and continued, "I and Juliandra would make sure Jeanie stays in line. We can't let the idiocy of these two bring bad name to us and destroy two homes."

Malvin and Josha looked at each other, and then Josha replied nodding in affirmative, "I guess that's the only way we are left with now."

"You are going to do no such thing," Jeanie exclaimed, "We are applying for a migration to US or Canada straight away."

"You are going nowhere that we don't want you to," Juliandra exclaimed as Malvin and Josha rushed forward to grab a lost Johnny, taking him with surprise. And as Jeanie tried to intervene, Juliandra and Sweena grabbed Jeanie and dragged her away. The two teens tried to resist, but were clearly overpowered by the combined might of those they weren't going to hurt.

"I'll get you Johnny, don't you worry," cried out a fighting Jeanie as her moms dragged her out of the room.

Arguments invariably lead to well reasoned decisions, but could also be a distraction when put forth with dishonest intentions. But once arguments have clarified a situation, the decisions left to be made are nothing more than foregone conclusions.

"Max told us what he was trying to do," Josha informed Johnny as the guards of metal and silicon escorted Johnny towards departure zone at the airport, "And now after what you have done here; I and Malvin have decided to give Max and his friends a free hand to deal with you."

Johnny however didn't respond to anything that was being said, perhaps sick of everything that had transpired over the last ten hours or so. He just dragged his feet along, as if going through the motions, possibly hoping it was all just a bad dream, or that something would just flip the entire situation on its' head.

"Are you going to say something you dumb head," Malvin too was equally disturbed by the flow of events thus far.

Johnny finally raised his head, and gave a really fierce look back to his fathers. They were just about to walk across a pedestrian crossing, to go to the section of the airport they needed to be at, but the situation really hadn't settled yet.

"Watch out," a pedestrian cried out as a car drove recklessly through the crowded zone shared by pedestrians and vehicles.

The car mercilessly hit the two robotic cops escorting Johnny, tossing them away and disassembling them in the process, and making Josha and Malvin move out of the way out of instinct.

"Get in," was the loud cry from Jeanie, as she pulled up right next to Johnny, and the passenger side door vanished to let him in. She was driving traceless, and time was of essence.

Jeanie Johnny

"Right or wrong is a classification dependent upon factors external to the subject and object involved."

Chapter Nine: Right enough

Dated: 31ˢᵗ August, 2118

What make up the yardstick to measure actions in a society, are the moral norms that a society collectively upholds. What that yardstick applies to, are acts and actors that may or may not fit or follow those cubicles of morality precisely.

Yet, the social morality determines whether what an individual thoughtfully characterised as right or wrong, will be described so by the remainder of the society. This is why courts have been in business since the beginning of all societies.

Societies however are anything but a homogenous cover of humanity above the earth. Differences of culture, religious affiliations, and so on so forth, have existed as long as societies themselves have existed in plural. Moral yardsticks have been known to encompass contrasting traits as acceptable, depending upon the two societies being compared. The distinction of right and wrong can not only merge but flip, as one leaves one society and moves into another. The only norms that manage to stay consistent across societies seem to be those that are bound by a more fundamental characteristic than mere choice of individuals making up a society; natural reason, as it could be described.

But when natural reasons are questioned, the norms can themselves become questionable. And when a society upholds questionable norms above and ahead of natural truths, the very foundations of such a society become prone to moral and structural erosion. What Johnny and

Jeanie refuse to accept as true, is an artificial norm that had somewhere down the timeline, emerged out of a society's very specific need. What however they have chosen to do, now threatens to tear apart the very foundations of that society.

"Are you alright," Jeanie asked Johnny, who had just jumped into the car, still caught in a daze of emotions and thoughts.

"What are we doing?" Johnny mumbled to himself, lost in thoughts somewhere remote than where he actually was; by Jeanie's side.

Jeanie may have flown her car in traceless, but the moment her vehicle had entered the perimeter of the airport, the sensors imbedded everywhere had picked up an unidentifiable vehicle, and were tracking her every move. The force field had already closed all entrance and exit points from the airport, and now it was rising up above the perimeter fast, to make escape impossible for any vehicle except an aircraft inside. Jeanie only had five minutes from the moment she entered the airport, and now the luxury had been reduced to a mere forty seconds.

"Hold on Johnny; we need to make this exit right now," Jeanie shouted out as she flew her car as fast as she could, dodging automated vehicles trying to hit hard and immobilize her vehicle. "Here we go," Jeanie exclaimed as she finally reached the perimeter and raised the car as high as she could. Luckily for her, she was a few microseconds early, and the car escaped outside safely.

"Woo!" Jeanie gave out a jubilant cry as she let go the joy-wheel, forgetting the auto-pilot had been disabled.

"Watch out," a scared Johnny freaked out as the car flew to the wrong side of the road and towards an approaching heavy vehicle.

"Oops! Sorry; I forgot," Jeanie apologized as she grabbed the controls again and dodged the incoming metal monster just in time. "Ok, listen to me carefully Johnny," Jeanie exclaimed as she saw police patrols shooting off in distance, in every direction and ready to pounce on the fugitives running away from law, "We are going to ditch my car in one of the side streets nearby, and then hop into a friend's waiting car. But I want you to remain totally silent and not utter a word anytime until we are outside the city bounds. Do you understand?"

"What?" a confused Johnny asked.

"Don't ask anything, just do as I say," Jeanie exclaimed as she made a quick run through the side-streets and alleys intersecting the residential blocks of the suburbs that lay by the side of the airport, "Get ready to jump on my call."

"What?" Johnny asked again, as if on an echo mode.

"Shush!" Jeanie silenced him as she released the force field doors, put her finger on the autopilot bypass switch, slowed down the car just enough to jump out with minor bruising, and then yelled, "Jump now!"

Johnny was about to utter another word but Jeanie shoved him out by force, and then getting ready to jump out herself, she quickly flicked the autopilot bypass off and yelled, "Get me home." And then, without giving the auto-pilot enough time to close all the doors, she bailed herself out too.

The duo fell hard on to the street below, rolling away towards different sides. But Jeanie quickly got onto her feet, and while Johnny got up brushing off dust, she rushed to him and put her hand hard on his mouth before he could utter a word. With a hard grasp of Johnny's other hand, Jeanie dragged him towards a car waiting by the kerb side a few meters away. She literally shoved Johnny into the back seat of the vehicle, and then jumped in behind him. Johnny was about to say something again, but she put her hand hard on his face again and pulled him down on the seat. Their driver didn't need any instructions, as she immediately pulled out and flew away.

Arousing are flights of fancy, fulfilling are dreams that materialize, satisfying are achievements, but compelling the calls of duty. Intelligent are those who convert their fancies' into their duty, for then fostering their passion becomes their job, and rewards become both achievements and fulfilled dreams.

"Yana, Gabriella; inside," the commissioner ordered two of her best detectives, to march into her office. As soon as they did so, the commissioner asked, "You are aware of the situation aren't you?"

"The girl that lifted a boy from the airport," Yana replied with a nod, "Heard she ditched her car somewhere and let the autopilot drag our auto-bots on a needless chase; intelligent and dim-witted at the same time."

"A rookie behind the trigger," Gabriella quipped, "Any sensible criminal would have known such an expansive heist won't take them far!"

"They are new young lovers damn it," the commissioner quipped, slapping her palm on the table in frustration, "And now it is a level four offence the bitch has committed and we will soon have media breathing down our necks."

"Airport I am sure was her choice out of desperation, but it sure works well for her," Yana agreed, and for good reasons, "Now people from across the globe would've already heard the news. Just think of all the nationalities that travel through our ports!"

"And that's why I am deputing the two of you on the case," the Commissioner looked straight into her girls' eyes, "Do what you have to, but I want the two kids alive and in, before they get to the media or across our borders."

"It might be easier to shoot them in their flight," Yana replied, "We have good reasons, and that would save us the massive issues and debates this one incident is going to stir." She then looked at her partner, in both senses of the word, and as if seeking her approval; she continued, "This case would put to question our entire way of life like none other has before."

"I'm sorry commissioner, but I beg to differ from my partner," Gabriella however replied, "We can't kill them, for that would be a media suicide, and the discussion that would flow out of it would be even worse."

"That girl has got assistance," Yana however argued, "She couldn't have pulled this stunt without some help. Every moment that we lose now, we are getting played out of this game."

"Correct as your evaluation appears to be Yana, it's your girl's call which is right," the Commissioner however replied back, "We have no choice but to get them alive."

"Only if we find them alive," was Yana's cryptic response.

"What do you mean?" the Commissioner was immediately suspicious.

"You leave that to me Ma'am," Yana replied with a confidence that made her partner shiver, as Gabriella stood their gaping.

Choice is married to decision, and decision married to imminent action. And since one cannot avoid taking some action or the other everyday in their lives, one cannot avoid making choices. Theoretically it means life altering decision could be made every day, but in practical experience, very few decisions actually have a potential to alter the course of one's life, even when they are major decisions. This happens because life is so complex, that many other decisions often combine to even out the effects of one life altering choice previously made. Thus for life to change course; a life altering decision has to be made consistently and repeatedly over an expanse of time.

"You are not going to let her in on this one, are you?" a concerned Gabriella asked as she followed hard behind her girlfriend and partner, Yana.

"Why ask questions that you already know the answer to?" Yana however replied with a question. But without waiting for an answer she whispered into her intelligent

wrist band, instructing it to make an encrypted call to an old ally.

Jeanie Johnny

"Time is neither short, nor enough, but as available!"

Chapter Ten: Rushed

Dated: 31st August, 2118

It's all about timing; the success. It is the precise moment that needs to be speared to ensnare the prize, for a moment more or less and the mark is lost. Time is never more than adequate, it is just what is available. Even when it appears there's plenty of time to spare, much of it only gets spared and decisions finalized in the dying moments.

Of course, the ambitious and industrious very easily manage to finish things with time to spare, but the battle then shifts to fighting the lull that could follow. Battles won with time to spare don't just end there. Those habitual of wining know this, which is why they don't rest on past accomplishments, including the one they just made a part of their past. Constant movement forward is the key to keep success alive and coming in.

Decisions will always have to be made in haste, for things are in constant flux in everyone's life; more so when important events are shaping up or happening. These are the decisions that one cannot dwell upon when amidst the whirlwind of activity. It's natural that not all decisions would look good when one would finally retrospect, but then one should remember; hindsight has the benefit of experience while foresight only had the benefit of reasoning. Jeanie and Johnny made a choice, and they too had some reasoning to back it up. But will their reasoning stand their own scrutiny; would be a test in time!

"This is my friend Alena Mathews," Jeanie finally introduced Johnny to their saviour, as soon as their vehicle had hit an outbound highway.

"My lady; you have guests that I don't identify," the car's intelligent system however interrupted, "Do I have your permission to identify your guests?"

"That won't be necessary, they are just friends; new friends," Alena replied to her car's intelligence system, "They are Sarah and Mitch. You can remember that."

"Thank you," the system responded and turned itself off.

Alena turned around, her eyebrows rolling over, as she finally greeted Johnny, "Hi Mitch, I and Sarah became friends very recently."

"Well thanks a lot Alena, for helping us," Johnny replied as he put his hand forward to shake Alena's hand, "It would be a favour hard to repay."

"Don't even need to mention that my friend," Alena replied, "Sarah literally owns my life now."

"No one owns anyone's life Alena," Jeanie however replied back, "I did what any good person would have done that day."

"In that case," Alena replied, "I am doing what any good friend should do! So don't feel indebted Mitch."

"Attention my lady," the car's system again interrupted their conversation, "An emergency transmission has been dispatched to all vehicles; to identify the people using them. I need your permission to identify your friends."

"I've already given you their identification," Alena yelled back, as if her tone would make any difference to a piece of software, but she continued in the same tone nevertheless, "Register the information as is!"

"I must advice you my lady; any information you provide to the authorities, is provided under oath to the Spirit-of-Justice, and any lies are punishable by Cryo-chamber terms," the car's intelligence system gave her the statutory warning before asking, "Do you agree to me registering the information as provided by you, that the occupants of this car are, by names; Alena, Sarah and Mitch?"

"Yes I agree," Alena however wasted no time in making her decision loud and clear.

"Can we stop somewhere," Johnny however was feeling suffocated and one could tell from his face, "I just want to step outside and take a few deep breaths of fresh air."

"As soon as we hit the international highway, we'll find a spot," Jeanie replied to him.

What makes a rollercoaster ride so thrilling is the impression it creates; that it is not going to stop anytime soon. What's edgy, when that also becomes unpredictable in tenure; the emotions experienced get raised to an altogether new level.

"I don't think we'll manage a positive identification through the system," Gabriella quipped as she quickly scanned the system compiled data, of passengers travelling via various means of transport.

"What's that," Yana, who was just about to brief the small team of handpicked officers assisting them in trace and capture, asked.

"The motorists and passengers identification system," Gabriella quipped, "If someone is assisting her, well aware of what she is doing, then that person won't give up true identity of passengers to the system."

"We'll just have to scan for abnormalities in data manually then," Yana knew what it meant to their chances of narrowing down upon the culprits at large, "Damn, that could take up to seven hours."

"We better get started straight away then," Gabriella quipped.

Science cannot replace human mind for science is the child of intellect. Sharper the science gets, sharper get the minds that develop it, and that learn it. The mind that creates is also the mind that questions 'what next'. It is this curiosity that keeps the mind ahead of its creation.

"Ok, what are we doing Jeanie," Johnny asked, shivering and freezing as the three of them were, standing outside in Alaskan autumn, far enough from Alena's car to escape its prying sensors.

"Well, here's the plan," Jeanie thought Johnny wanted to know where they were going, "Everybody would expect us to sneak across into US state of New British Colombia, but we are rather going to make a sharp left about four eighty miles from here, and then cross over into Canada."

"That's not what I meant Jeanie," Johnny however had something else weighing down upon his heart, "What I mean is; do we know what we are doing?"

His question may not have surprised Jeanie, but it sure made her eyes moist, "Do you think I like the situation that we are in?"

"You don't need to say that to me," Johnny replied as he pulled out his hands from his pocket and took her face in his hands softly. Her face was really cold, with wind blowing miniscule snow crystals onto it. Her skin was pale as if all blood had dried inside her. Yet her beauty looked other-worldly. "What we are doing is not just something out of the ordinary for our societies," Johnny continued, "But it is out of ordinary for ourselves. And then, we have those that we have loved more than our own lives, on the other side of the firing line."

"I don't know what to do Johnny," Jeanie cried, "Four days ago my life was so different. I agree I didn't like it for some reason, but it was liveable and predictable." As tears rolled down her cheeks, she looked into Johnny's eyes, "Then out of nowhere you marched straight into it, and now I don't know anymore what is right or what is wrong." She paused for Johnny to answer, but Johnny himself didn't know what to say. So she asked him, "Tell me Johnny; is there any other alternative that you would rather have than what we have chosen for us?"

Her question made Johnny take a deep breath, as the situation seemed to fall in place on its' own. He finally had an answer, "You are right Jeanie. You are the first girl in my life that has made me realize what I had been seeking all my life." With a new found strength he looked Jeanie in her eyes and continued, "Living without you is quite a thing of another level, I am not even ready to go back to my old life anymore, were someone to offer me a one way trip back in time." The duo took a deep breath before Johnny continued, "We have nothing to be ashamed of for we are correct by all natural reasons. Artificial reasoning is not going to create a wedge between us; at least not without killing me." And he grabbed Jeanie hard in his embrace as the duo kissed each other with passion, the wind around them literally set alight.

Certain emotions are forged in fire, the one that burns inside a human heart. These are the emotions that are tied to intense passions; like lust, greed, and vengeance. Happiness, likes and dislikes, and fears, they are much shallower; originating outside the hearts, somewhere in minds, even though they eventually flow into and fill up the heart.

"I knew it," exclaimed Crystal as her subordinate confirmed that Alena's car was missing from her house, and she hadn't rocked up to her work either, "That bitch is the only person who could help Jeanie in this."

"Then what are we waiting for," the subordinate jubilantly exclaimed, "What better opportunity do we need to settle two scores at once!"

"Let's get the beast on road Rosy," Crystal replied before turning her attention to the crazy geek of their band, "And you Julie; babe you get me into the transport network by any means possible, and get me where the bitch is heading right now."

"Why not just ask that uniformed bitch of yours," asked the crazy geek Julie, "That will save us a lot of time."

"And gift away my only chance to teach that bitch the last lesson of her life; no way," Crystal quipped in rage, "We'll call those bitches in blue once we have bagged the bodies."

Jeanie Johnny

"Love is a risk that even great minds take."

Chapter Eleven: Out of my way

Dated: 31st August, 2118

easoning and love don't share the same bed. What use is the foresight of logic when controls are being commandeered by a blindfolded intellect? Emotions are not designed to beg, but rather demand. It's sensibility which knows the difference between need and desire, and how to swap the two according to changing circumstances. For emotions, circumstances are immaterial and only results matter. On the other hand, sensibility is about determining both actions and results according to the call of the circumstances.

Indeed many would argue that one often regrets those decisions most, that they made against their heart's wishes. But how many of those regretful ones would rather live their lives again the other way? Perhaps not too many! On closer introspection, every hard reasoned decision turns out to be the best choice made, that helped in achieving stability in life in the longer run. Of course, there would always be those who only made bad decisions based on bad reasoning, but then that is generally love.

But of course, love does not necessarily have to drive everyone towards self-destruction, for, like any other eventuality in life, even love can hit one as the best possible probability. Even love could bring opportunities that any other choice may not have provided an individual in the circumstances of the time. Rare as such occurrences might be; some people do get to live their fairytales. They are generally the people who know how to identify a fairytale romance from amongst the muck of life. Can

Jeanie and Johnny be one such lucky couple, is however for time to disclose.

"I'm so hungry," Johnny exclaimed as he saw another 'Fenaline's Place' being left behind.

"So am I," Jeanie exclaimed.

"Are you sure you want to invest some time in gluttony right now?" Alena asked the duo, reminding them the importance of time.

"I know it's a bad idea, but I'm so thirsty as well," Jeanie exclaimed as she looked towards Johnny. She then asked Alena, "How much distance is left to be covered?"

"About two hundred miles more to go," Alena replied, "Barely a forty minute flight in this one, but one that could also take ages, if you get the drift."

"I am about to burst as well," Johnny exclaimed.

"That's exactly what I wanted to say," Jeanie exclaimed.

"How about you guys take two minutes behind that snow mound," Alena finally made the choice for them, "I'll just get you something in that time."

"Brilliant," exclaimed Johnny as he wasted no time in hopping out of the car as it came to a stop.

Brilliance is not in the diamond, but in the hands of the craftsman that gives it precise cuts. The same diamond may turn out to be a barely noticeable piece of rock when coming out of the hands of a novice. The professional knows how hard to cut, and at what angle.

"Why would anyone as sharp as this bitch, make such an obvious exit choice?" Yana asked, as her frustration grew with each passing moment. Three and a half hours of manual scavenging of vehicular data coming out of 'US New British Columbia' route hadn't yielded any results.

"I can see your point," Gabriella quipped, "Maybe we should start scavenging the data for other international routes that the bitch might consider."

"If it was me, I would drive towards the US New British Colombia border post, just so to drive the authorities in that direction," Yana thoughtfully commented as her mind went into overdrive, bringing up arguments, "But cut away at any one of these five points that lead towards YT Canada."

"Perhaps we need to scan the data coming out of vehicles traversing those roads," Gabriella too was in absolute agreement on this one.

Plan is the starting point of a solution, even though the fight might have started much earlier than when one is finally put in place. But while that initial fight is all about survival, once a plan is put in place, the fight also becomes about salvaging all that can be saved.

"Thank you," Alena acknowledged the silicon-aluminium beauty minding the delivery window at the fast food drive thru. She then quickly drove out, to head back in direction she was supposed to be traversing with her friends. However, they had finally run out of easy time.

"Get the bitch," yelled Crystal on top of her voice as Rosy pressed hard on the monster truck's accelerator.

"What the hell," taken by surprise but unaware of the new company, Alena twisted her car's joy-wheel with purpose adequate enough for a life on line. She managed to dodge direct impact, but took a few moments more than needed to bring the vehicle back on intended track. In the meantime Rosy had spun the monster truck around, to face Alena's car head on.

"Crush her," yelled Crystal and others as Rosy accelerated hard and straight towards Alena.

Left with no choice or direction better than a clean escape, Alena however pressed on the accelerator herself, and headed straight for a head on impact. Luckily however, she still had her wits around her. At the very last moment, having carefully observed Rosy's reactions behind her joy-wheel, she swung hard and high to a side, avoiding a direct impact, and racing away. The time it took Rosy to turn around, there was already a big lead to catch up to.

"The brazen bitches are here," Alena yelled out to Johnny and Jeanie as soon as she stopped by the side of the road, "Rush, we don't have time!"

The duo rushed towards the car, but alas, Crystal's beast was quicker than them. The impact was massive enough to toss poor Alena's car many meters high in the sky, and many meters beyond along the road. Alena's car rolled over and over before it finally came to a halt on its side, with Alena's lifeless body hanging out of the door.

"Kill 'em," Crystal yelled out again to Rosy, but fortunately for Johnny and Jeanie, the accident's impact had rendered Crystal's monster immobile for good.

"I can't," Rosy exclaimed as she tried everything she could, to get the beast moving again, before finally giving up, "It is dead!"

"Run Jeanie," Johnny yelled as he grabbed Jeanie's hand, and made a dash towards the direction they were supposed to be heading in.

"Don't let the bastards get away," yelled Crystal as she and her band hopped out of their dead vehicle and rushed behind the duo, lasers flashing in their hands.

A perfect get away is the one from one's own dark side. It is the side which never leaves a person alone, not even in

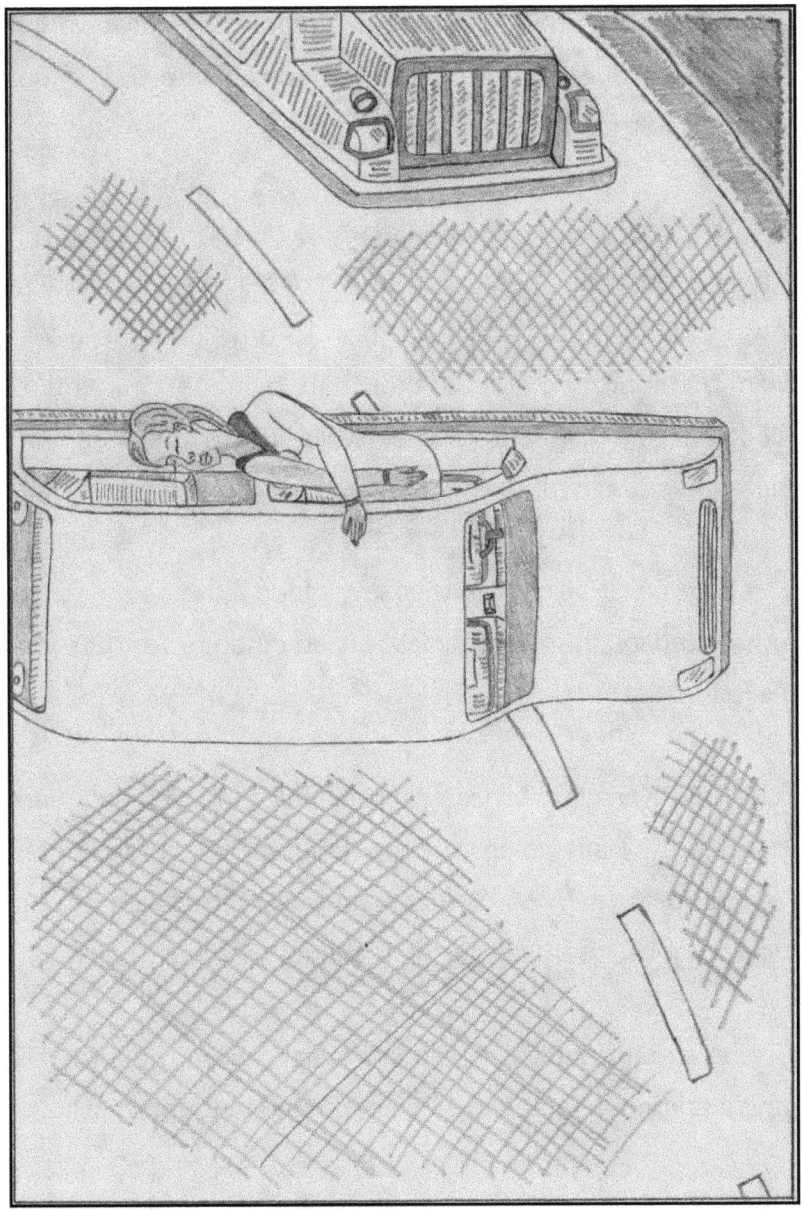

their sleep. The passions it stirs, the prejudices it raises, the greed it fosters; everything about it is overpowering, that bears down upon a person's conscience until it has consumed their life and happiness.

The New York traffic had been as bad this day as it had grown notorious to be. But in a connected world where even one's breaths were not private anymore, there was one band of delinquents that had become masters of dodging half the authorities, while the other half was humane and corrupt.

"Tenzer, did you get the news feed," the voice at the other end of the communication channel in Tenzer's car asked.

"I did Karson," Tenzer replied, "We need to get there right away! I am going to send Taila a SOS, to arrange a vehicle for us in WFA. You get the rest of the team moving and meet me at the airport in ten. I got the seats booked."

"We may need your brother's help," Karson replied, "His unit's stationed near the YT Canada and WFA border."

"You have worked the correct preferable exit, but the situation is too volatile to count all our chooks before they hatch," Tenzer however wasn't keen on Karson's suggestion, "He can really end our flight even before we leave the New York port."

"Things have a potential of going horribly wrong on this one," Karson however had his worries, "This is exactly the situation that our brothers and sisters have been trying to create for the past fifty years. We can't miss this chance!"

"Yes, but we can't let the 'Global Defence Force' get a whiff of our plans until we accomplish what we want," Tenzer replied, "Most particularly my brother; he's dead against our endeavours."

"But we may need his help," Karson however had concerns, "That place is like a minefield, given the work we intend to do."

"He would be a roadblock if anything, and any tip off to 'Global Defence Force' would end our mission even before it starts," Tenzer replied, "I know my brother; a straight by the book army man, while GDF is openly and directly opposed to the work of 'Nature's Warriors Against Immorality'. They won't even let us fly out if either of them gets a whiff of what we are up to."

"But there may not be any guarantees of escape this time," Karson however was more concerned about what he could foresee as consequences of their intended action.

"My brother will be my last resort," Tenzer replied, "The one I'll call just before taking my last breath."

Jeanie Johnny

"Only a coward panics the same twice."

Chapter Twelve: Ominous words

Dated: 31ˢᵗ August, 2118

Fear is natural and complex. It is complex for it is a mixture of surprise, desire, and need or greed; surprise at the materialization of the unexpected, desire to have a result other than what might then happen, and either a pressing need or compelling greed, to seek the desired result. And the fact that all these individual emotions are as much a part of an intellectual being as much a dumb beast; makes fear a universally experienced phenomenon.

Every human and beast thus knows what a panic attack is, for everyone has experienced this draining, sinking feeling at some point in their life. The only thing that makes a strong individual brave-heart, and the weak a coward, is the difference in training. The first experience teaches an individual not only how panic sets in and what it feels like, but also, how panic makes individuals make sorry choices, and more importantly, how things generally don't turn out as bad as feared in a state of panic. The brave don't yield to fear again, while a coward never learns how to face it!

Those who master their emotions, master them completely when fear is their slave. They are the people who don't need to look behind, for they know they are too fast for the past to catch up. They are the people who don't stop and give up at the first sign of trouble, for they are too trained to be trapped by an unknown future. Jeanie and Johnny are definitely two people who don't identify fear as an issue, for else they wouldn't be where they find themselves today.

"Get the bitch and the bastard," Crystal yelled as she stopped in her stride to take a laser shot, only to miss another one as Johnny and Jeanie changed their direction once again.

"We can't outrun them for too long Johnny," a concerned Jeanie exclaimed as she looked back and caught a glimpse of fast catching up Rosie and Julie, with Crystal and two others only a bit further behind.

"I know, but keep running for," Johnny replied as he took a quick glance behind, "One more step."

"What," a surprised Jeanie turned her head to look at him, but by that time she was at least three steps too far ahead.

Johnny had turned around in a flash, and lunged in the air to land two mean punches, one each in the face of Rosy and Julie. Blood from their torn lips got splattered across the ice, as the two tumbled on to their backs. The three others tried to stop in their stride and take aim at the advancing Johnny, but Johnny was too quick for them. He dived low and, with one kick below her knees, lifted Crystal up in the air and towards an incoming Jeanie, who had just landed a couple of quick mean hits each to the heads of the two girls knocked down by Johnny earlier. A big one right in the middle of Crystal's face was enough to down her for good.

The other two tried to focus their handguns on Johnny, but not only the boy was quickly right in the middle of the two, but also faster than a chimp in jumping away at the same time. Meanwhile Jeanie too finally got the chance to pullout her own handgun, and with two quick shots, she disarmed the duo. Johnny finished the game with a bully punch to one's head, and a massive kick in the other's ribs. The two went down in no time, and Johnny made sure a punch each to their heads knocked them out for the time.

"You killed my friend you bitch," Jeanie however had very quickly turned into an extremely enraged and ferocious looking girl, and was standing right above a thoroughly beaten Crystal, "Now die bitch!"

"No, no, don't shoot," Johnny dived to pull Jeanie away from Crystal, barely quick enough to make the laser shot miss Crystal's head by a whisker. "Please Jeanie, don't," Johnny pleaded, "We are no murderers!"

"But she killed my friend," Jeanie broke down, "She killed our saviour!"

"I know," Johnny took her face in his palms, tears rolling down his eyes, "But I also know; it's not something Alena would want us to do!" And Jeanie broke down in Johnny's arms.

Rosy, who had finally gathered her wits together, saw her chance and quickly grabbed a gun to take a shot.

"No," yelled a broken, bruised, and shaken Crystal, "Don't!"

Johnny and Jeanie turned around and looked at Rosy, and then Crystal, with questions filling up their eyes.

"There are untraceable bikes in the back of the beast," a very changed Crystal exclaimed to Jeanie and Johnny, "It would take barely ten minutes for emergency crews to arrive here, and your friend's car would have sent an SOS the moment our vehicle hit her. You only have three or four minutes to move out."

The questions might not have been answered, and perhaps Jeanie would have loved to say something, or maybe perhaps nothing was need to be said anymore, but silence triumphed nevertheless. Jeanie and Johnny gave a slight nod with their heads, and rushed back to Crystal's monster truck. True to Crystal's words, there were three bikes in the back of the beast, and they only needed, and took, one!

The toughest part of trying to understand another human is determining how much of that human can be trusted. Long term relations don't suffer from trust issues because people get used to the level of risks involved in dealing with a person. Familiarity is comforting when it comes to relationships, for one is familiar with the dogs that bark, and dogs that can potentially bite.

"That's it, that has to be the car," Gabriella yelled as she identified the information supplied by Alena's car as inaccurate, "The names given by Miss Mathews' car don't add up to our database of individuals inside WFA at this moment."

"You might want to check this out," Yana however had some other information to share, "A car had been in a major accident on International Highway 41; no survivors detected." She looked at Gabriella's face to watch her expressions at the last bit of information, "It was Alena's vehicle."

"Could be an act of," Gabriella immediately knew whose handiwork that might have been, and sunk in her chair dejected at the outcome, "Shit!"

"It'll be fine babe," Yana quipped as she jumped out of her seat and walked up to her partner. She put her hand on dejected Gabriella's shoulder and quipped, "We need to confirm the kill. Let's go!"

In an entangled complex situation; what is good for one, is bound to be bad for another. The question, as to whether the good happened to the one who was righteous, or not, is only just another layer of inspection. All that's really left there to scavenge is the learning.

"Oh my god, I can't believe this," a terrified Sweena exclaimed as the two couples huddled around the Virtual-Vision set, watching the live news feed of the events that had just transpired.

"I don't believe this," a distraught Malvin too exclaimed, with pain writ large on his face, "Who doesn't know the kind of scumbags that roam the streets in our towns; the maniacs and psychopaths."

"How did this end up like this," Josha quipped as he grabbed his head in his hands in despair, "If only you could've held on to Jeanie and not let her escape."

"We couldn't have kept her chained, least of all, forever," an equally distraught Juliandra let out a cry drenched in pain, "She's a lioness that can't be tamed."

"She broke free the moment we dragged her outside the airport detention, and never gave us a chance to catch a hold of her again," a sobbing Sweena added, "If only we knew what she was up to; we would have alerted the authorities and none of this would have happened."

"There's only one body at the scene," the news reporter at the sight was continuing with her information, "And while the police question the 'Brazen Babes' regarding the remaining occupants of the ill-fated vehicle, suspected to be the two young fugitives, the girls have refused to talk without an attorney."

"Wait guys!" and Malvin immediately latched on to the little sign of hope that emerged out of the situation, "Our kids might still be alive."

Hope breathes harder and faster than life. While life is prone to despair, hope fights against it.

"Are we going to continue on this track," a concerned Johnny asked as he sped the bike hard forward, about twenty miles down from the accident site.

"No," Jeanie replied as she clung hard to him, ridding pillion, "We must go right at the next bend."

"Sure; but where to," Johnny asked.

"We'll have to head down to US New British Colombia now," Jeanie quipped, "They are going to lock down all five way-outs this side, and raise the force field across the border belt. Then they will scavenge this entire zone in our search. We need to get back to the track that they won't expect us to be on right now, and hope that they don't so too soon either."

Her words made Johnny pause as a concern grew on his face, "But that means we won't be able to get out very soon."

"Not for another eight hours I suppose," Jeanie knew they had lost precious time.

Johnny took a deep breath and then asked, "Remember what Alena had said when we had jumped out of her car back there."

"I do," a contemplative Jeanie nodded in affirmation.

Jeanie Johnny

"When life is intent to go places, roads are discovered where none exists."

Chapter Thirteen: Race to destiny

Dated: 1ˢᵗ September 2118

Blessed are those who are never satisfied with their achievements, and blessings are what they bring to the rest. The desire to create something better, achieve something better, or indulge in something better, keeps driving their appetite for accomplishments.

The enterprising achieve success, but their success invariably touches many more lives than those directly connected to them. Such is the entanglement of economy; one section or individual cannot succeed without the benefits trickling down into other sections of it. The entrepreneurs build nations!

True it is that this blessing, like any other, could also become a bane, when prejudices clamp the base of work. Much blood has been shed on this earth, at the command of some such hard to reason entrepreneurs of various eras and communities. But then such curses of humanity were eventually brought down by equally enterprising good people, and humanity learnt. Enterprises never become a bigger problem than those who offer solutions, for every problem is that much more a motivation for the solution seeking entrepreneurs.

Tough thus is, to contain the exuberance of those who seek adventure, for they are not bound by maps and guided by mazes of roads. They find their own ways to succeed, and roads appear where and when there were none earlier. Johnny and Jeanie have found many for themselves so far, but their flight is far from over just yet.

"We need to make it across before the daybreak," Jeanie exclaimed as she clung on tighter to Johnny, freezing in the Alaskan refrigerator on a glide-bike. There was only so much warmth the four hot air vents could have provided the two riders, for the pace of journey was too fast. If it were not for the weather conditioned gloves and helmets, some of their extremities could have easily fallen off by now.

"Trust me love, I'm on to it," Johnny exclaimed, "Just let me know if I hit the wrong way, and four hours would fly away like mist."

Mist of ignorance is thickest when one refuses to accept the light of reason and thinnest when knowledge shines bright on it. A reasoned argument is the initiating point of progress. Without it; one is only gambling with probabilities.

"Get me the news update Ronario," Tenzer gave some quick directions to his team, as they made their way out of the 'Arrivals' section at the airport, and towards a waiting Talia, "There she is; Talia." And the team rushed out to her.

"Hello boys," Talia greeted them all as a single lot, and without wasting time on formalities, cut straight to the point, "We have no time to lose. Follow me!"

"What are you providing us?" Tenzer asked as they quick marched to a waiting limousine.

"Much more than what you asked," Talia replied, "Let's first get outside the airport zone."

What one needs, is a very time dependent query. One's needs at any given point may not be the same as what they want generally in their life. Necessity is about short term requirements; the loose change of needs.

"Only one body recovered at the scene," Gabriella informed Yana, as their turbo-powered vehicle razed across the roads and towards an unknown direction.

"Any word from the airborne teams; have they come across any vehicles yet," Yana asked as she herself scrolled through the data of all the vehicles travelling in either direction on 'International Highway 41'.

"The senior pilot just pushed an update," Gabriella replied as she checked the data on her device, "There's no vehicle of any description travelling down that road at this hour."

"They've changed course," Yana didn't need to think twice about that call.

"US NBC perhaps," Gabriella made the suggestion.

Yana didn't need to answer, but only a wink was enough.

The knowledge of what will happen may not really come as a gift from the clairvoyant, but could rather be, and most often is, the common sense of a reasoned being. When one is aware of all the factors involved, and all or most of the possible outcomes; any intelligent being can determine the most likely outcome. Of course one may subconsciously overlook the one they don't want to accept, but then they risk an unwanted result at their own peril.

"We can't just ride across the border, don't you think," Johnny asked.

"We might have to hitch a ride somewhere before that," Jeanie replied.

"And how exactly are we going to manage that," Johnny asked the obvious.

"I don't know," Jeanie exclaimed, and then paused for a second before making a very weird statement, "You know there's a river that flows not far from this road."

"No way," Johnny immediately knew what she was going to suggest, "It is freaking cold, and we'll freeze to our deaths before we even make ten miles beyond."

"Do you have any other idea," Jeanie asked.

Johnny was left speechless for all practical purposes, were one to exclude his meek response, "Can I think over it?"

One has to really be a step ahead of life, to achieve a much cherished goal. Those who wait for curve balls, spend most of their time preparing to tackle them only. Those who succeed however, they also prepare to milk the balls that follow the curve balls.

"This crap doesn't show a thing," a frustrated Gabriella quipped as she went about flipping away screen after screen of data, and yet not getting the speck she was looking for.

"Wait, I see something on the road," Yana however caught a glimpse of a tiny light flying somewhere through the windy sheets of ice, "Looks like a glide-bike."

"There's nothing on my screen," Gabriella however had nothing on the satellite data in front of her.

"Bingo! We got them," Yana let out a victorious cheer, and then turned to her colleague behind the joy-wheel, "Mindy; get me close." And then she turned to her other sub-ordinate officer, "And you Becky; get ready to light them up."

The bright headlight of their glide-bike had betrayed the lovers in the black of the night, barely a hundred miles from their exit. It was literally heartache two within twenty four hours for them; and the shock came when a bright flare shot off into the air from behind, lighting up a ten mile radius as if daytime had arrived a few hours too early.

"What is that," a shocked Jeanie asked, but Johnny didn't need to answer her query. The police siren broke the silence of the serene night, and signalled their presence loud and clear.

"Shit, we are caught Johnny," Jeanie expectedly freaked out, "Do something; please do something."

"Not so easy babe," a determined Johnny however replied, "Not till I am alive." And he twisted the devil's ear as much as he could.

"Really," quipped Mindy, in a near sadistic tone.

"Let's give the kid a short demo," Yana too smiled at the youth's impetuosity, "Becky, keep all your flares handy. We might need a few more of them."

The chase was on, and the handicap the lovebirds were playing with, became too obvious when the second flare added to and extended the glow of the long burning previous flare. Soon the cop truck was flying parallel to them. Yana looked through the side window, at Johnny's face behind the visor, and when Johnny turned his head to look at her, she made sure she puckered her lips at him in the creepiest and most condescending of fashions.

But Johnny, if he was neck deep in trouble, he had already drowned in love. Nothing but death could have stopped him now, and that he was prepared to risk it all, became all too apparent when he made a sharp turn away from the road, and drove across the snow covered terrain.

"Which way is the river," he asked Jeanie.

"The other way," Jeanie replied, not sure what Johnny was up to.

Meanwhile Mindy had turned the vehicle around and driven off the road herself, hot in pursuit of the lovebirds.

"Hand me the Long-Bone 24," Yana instructed Becky.

"What," a shocked Gabriella exclaimed, fear lit large in her eyes, "You are not going to kill them are you?"

"Nope," Yana quipped, "Just clip their wings." She then looked at Mindy, "Get me a clear shot of their power-base."

"Sure," Mindy quipped just as Johnny swung his bike around once more, to head towards the river.

The lover rode ferociously, but his equipment was clearly underpowered and outclassed. Mindy didn't need much time to line up a clean shot for Yana, and Yana wasn't the one known for missing opportunities. Her shot was clean, and the sniper gun capable enough, to destroy the internals of the bike's power-base, rendering it immobile.

Johnny did lose control, and the bike took more than a tumble, but the lovers hadn't yet lost the fight. The two quickly got onto their feet, and made a hopeless run for it.

"Stop," ordered Yana, and stop is what Mindy did. "Lift me up," Yana instructed further as she stood on a platform in the back cabin of the police vehicle. Mindy confirmed the command to the vehicle's system, and the platform rose up and out of an opening in the roof. Gabriella and others too joined her on the vehicle's roof top.

"Relay my voice loud and clear," Yana instructed Mindy, who complied. "Listen, Johnny and Jeanie; there's nowhere to run, and I give you three seconds to stop, or I will blow your legs away," Yana's commanding voice roared across the open terrain.

"Oh my god, what do we do," a panicked Jeanie asked Johnny.

"She's bluffing," Johnny quipped and then asked, "But do you want to give up just like that?"

The duo stopped for a second, looked into each other's eyes, and then with a resolve tougher than steel, grabbed each other's hand and made a dash again.

"Are you kidding me," a shocked Yana quipped, but she was already at the end of her tether, and immediately raised her Long-Bone 24.

"No don't," Gabriella however pushed the muzzle away just in time, "We don't need to! They can't get anywhere from here."

"Don't," Yana wanted to say something, but her words were left hanging in her mouth as one after the other five shots of sniper fire rained on her team. The first one blew open Gabriella's torso, as her lifeless body was flung away

and off the vehicle. Three others left Yana team less, while the fourth one barely missed killing her as her Long-Bone's barrel deflected it away.

"Gabriella," a distraught Yana let out a cry for her dead partner, as another volley of shots hit her vehicle, while she barely escaped by diving down to the ground below.

"What the hell is that?" a shocked Johnny exclaimed as he looked behind, and then forward, and then towards Jeanie.

"Jeanie, Johnny," an unknown voice sought their attention; from just a few yards away, "This way now, if you want to live."

Jeanie Johnny

"Humility is for cows; lions are just majestic."

Chapter Fourteen: Thump down

Dated: 1ˢᵗ September, 2118

Some people are just like that, in your face; take it or leave it. They are those who say things as they see them, speak words as they think them, and treat others how their heart tells them to. They are the people either one likes, or one doesn't. And then there are those who know how to soften, blunt, or defang their words before their mind instructs their tongues to utter them. They are very easy to like, at least initially. But even they don't create every bond to last a lifetime, for the roses may hide a dagger, but they can't save its' cuts.

Some people's work is like that too; in your face when one witnesses it. Such works may either bowl one over, or blow their fuse, but they remain what they always were; unpretentious. These are the works that cannot be ignored, and when one notices them, they either leave one speechless by their brilliance, or burnt inside out. They are the works that would never be humble, neither in content, nor in appearance, or in their claim to glory. Such works, like such people, are lions that don't look humble even when taking a leisurely stroll through the forest. They were born majestic; they live majestic; and will always appear majestic.

Humility is for cows that fear the shepherd won't take them to the grass, or a predator won't let them feed. Such are those people who live their lives fearing they would lose what they have achieved. They are the people who may be the masters of their art, yet are not masters of their minds; weaklings that survived the struggle yet fear lest they have to do it again. Humility is neither in the work of

Yana, nor Tenzer, yet either's work cannot survive the other's; what a shame!

"Do we know you," Johnny asked the unknown lady calling out their names, as the light of the two long lasting flares finally started to grow out.

"We'll have plenty of time for introductions in the vehicle," the lady replied, as four others', three men and another lady, kept their Long-Bone 24s trained at the ambushed vehicle.

"Quick, no time to waste," yelled the other lady in the pack.

Johnny and Jeanie didn't have the luxury of options even if they were wary; of their company, of trusting this mixed bunch welcoming party. However two shots flew past their frames, barely missing one man in the pack.

"One's alive," yelled the other lady, to caution everybody.

"Into the vehicles quick," yelled the first lady again, as more shots flew past the group, targeting their vehicles, "The bitch will destroy them otherwise."

"Go, go, go," yelled the leader of the pack, as he and the two other men in the group fired at will, just to distract the sniper at the other end. This time Johnny and Jeanie paid heed, and rushed into one of the two big vans.

"Tenzer, off you go now," Deezer yelled as soon as Talia had secured Jeanie and Johnny in one van with her, while the other lady rushed to man the other vehicle, with Ronario by her side.

"Get in Deezer," Ronario yelled as Talia manned van took off. But Yana is not the one that lets' her prey escape so lightly. The moment Deezer turned his back to get into the second van; his head was there no more above his shoulders. The loss shook Ronario for a bit, but the girl behind the joy-wheel knew what was needed, and pressed the paddle.

As soon as Yana saw the vehicles moving away, she rushed back to her own damaged vehicle. She pulled Mindy's lifeless body out of the pilot seat and hopped in to try and get the vehicle rolling again, but realized straightaway, she needed a new ride. She then rushed into the back cabin, picked up Becky's flare gun, and shot two flares, to light up the skies. She then quickly pulled out a wide spectrum guided binoculars from the dashboard compartment, raised the emergency alarm, buckled herself into the driver seat in an uncomfortable sideways position, and pressed the eject button.

The seat was flung high up into the air, with Yana ready to grab her chance with both hands. She immediately locked her binoculars on to the fleeing vehicles, and with a press of a button, their identification numbers were copied and beamed back to the control room.

"Yana to base," she yelled into her intelligent wristband, "Disable these vehicles immediately, and I need a backup team on site straight away."

Meanwhile the two escape vehicles pushed on hard towards the international border.

"Call your brother," Talia suggested to Tenzer, "There's no way we'll get out of this place without his help."

"Not yet," a stubborn Tenzer however replied, "Not until we are only one mile from the border. I don't want him to stop our mission right here."

"Sorry to interrupt you guys, but who are you and what mission are you talking about," Johnny asked, for he and Jeanie were desperately in need of some answers.

"To save you," Tenzer quipped, albeit patronizingly, "We are here just to save you."

"Thanks a lot guys but who are you?" Johnny however wasn't impressed, "And why, of course?"

"As to why; let us say we support a particular life style, the way of nature," Tenzer replied to his queries, "And as to who; we are the 'Nature's Warriors Against Immorality'."

His words left both Johnny and Jeanie speechless. It was one shadowy organisation, much maligned for its campaign against homosexual communities, and its active support to subversive acts in both 'Women's Federation of Alaska' and 'Southern Frontier Union'. Yet here they were, right in the middle of their assets, looking for safety.

"Shit, we've been tracked down," a panicked Talia informed, "Our vehicle will seize in ten seconds. Brace for shock!"

It seemed like this journey was not going to end anytime soon for Johnny and Jeanie, as both the vehicle involved in taking them out of WFA, jammed in the middle of nowhere. In fact, had Talia and the other girl not applied emergency brakes to slow down their speed, the vehicles could have easily rolled over for a mile or two, potentially killing all on board.

"Out of the vehicles, quick," Tenzer quipped as the group blew away the intentionally jammed doors with their lasers. "Give me something good to latch on to Talia," Tenzer asked Talia.

"Miranda is carrying a powered raft," Talia replied, "There's a river four hundred yards away, that crosses the border bisecting the force-field. With current adding to our speed, we'll barely lose five minutes."

"Off to the river," was Tenzer's direction without hesitation, and everybody knew what was to be done. Tenzer however continued, "They will definitely detect our footprints in snow, and will follow us downstream, no doubt. But we can easily kill a lot of miles and hop out where they least expect us to."

"Sounds like a great plan," Ronario quipped, "We should have clear ten minutes before the backup police team gets to this spot. We better move quickly!"

With a nice plan figured on the run, the six of them, including Johnny and Jeanie, made a dash towards the river.

"If we only had three hover boards in our equipment, this would have been a lot easier," Miranda quipped as she shouldered the heaviest baggage of all.

"It's not a mile away," chided Talia, as she herself balanced more than a Long-Bone 24 on her shoulder. She was also carrying the Multi-Strip-Lever, just like Tenzer and Ronario.

"Do you guys need any help?" Johnny asked.

"Nope," quipped Tenzer as the group made quick work of the four hundred yards.

By the edge of the cliff they stopped, where Ronario and Tenzer quickly programmed their Multi-Strip-Levers. A beam of solid light emerged out Ronario's lever, and got hooked to the barrel end of Tenzer's equipment.

"Off I go," Tenzer quipped as he jumped down the cliff, with Ronario's lever extending out the light beam like a rope, at a healthy pace. Within five seconds Tenzer had descended three hundred feet safely.

"You latch on to Talia," Ronario quipped to Jeanie as he maintained the light way extending between his device and Tenzer's.

Jeanie latched on to Talia's body, as Talia used her Multi-Strip-Lever to create a light hook, and attached it to the already established light way. She jumped down along with Jeanie, and reached the ground safely like Tenzer. With a flick of a button, Talia's device got pulled back up to Ronario, who motioned Johnny to cling on to Miranda, and the duo followed Talia and Jeanie's example.

With everybody else down, Ronario let go his Multi-Strip-Lever, which was quickly pulled down by Tenzer's device. Then, using the three levers, Talia, Tenzer and Miranda created a light sheet for Ronario to jump into safely. Once everybody was down, Miranda opened her backpack, and pulled out a folded piece of equipment. The moment she put the equipment piece in water, its intelligent system became operational and it folded itself out into a raft.

"Quick, hope into it," Tenzer motioned Jeanie and Johnny, and that is what they did, followed by everybody else.

Miranda didn't waste any time in starting the power system, and very soon the raft was literally flying across the river at a fearsome speed; guided by satellite navigation for path, and total area radio scan for obstacle identification.

Meanwhile Yana, who had been picked up by a backup team, wasted no time to reach the spot where the escape vehicles had ceased motion.

"They look perfect," Yana quipped the moment she saw the state of the vehicles, "Quick, we need to search their tracks. They will most likely head to the river."

Those who had however given a slip, wanted to make sure they didn't lose their advantage in time.

"We need to get off at least seven miles before we hit the border," Tenzer explained to his companions, "The border force would have already been alerted, and they might not just have prepared for a river exit, but we might even run into a pre-emptive patrol party."

"What if we bump into one much earlier," Talia asked.

"Then we use the guns," Tenzer replied, "Else we jump out, let the raft float off at natural speed, and climb up to the top of the cliff again."

"Which side ridge would it be?" Ronario asked.

"The same side as before," Tenzer replied, "We'll cross the border somewhere off-track, and I'll connect to my brother one mile short of it."

"It won't be easy running through that thick snow," Johnny had his fears.

"Take heart boy, from the fact that the distance by land from where we get off, would be only five miles," Tenzer chided him in reply.

That urgency was the only thing that could save them, was a foregone conclusion, but their work wasn't easy. Running even five miles in snow takes a hell lot of time, strength, and stamina, especially if you are not trained to run. They jumped off the raft according to the plan, and made quick work climbing up and getting on the move. Their speed however was but a subject of their slowest member.

"Oh C'mon Jeanie, you haven't even got a gun to carry," Talia complained as she made the rear end of the band running under the moon light.

"I'm sorry, but I am doing my best," a huffing and puffing Jeanie replied.

However, before a word more could have been uttered, and barely one mile from the border, the first shot silenced Talia once and for all.

"Shit, they've tracked us," Tenzer quipped as he turned around to face the fast approaching police team.

Ronario fired the first shots of resistance, followed by an enraged Miranda, but a volley flew back from the other end, as the police team split into five groups of turbo-charged super-bikes.

Having realized the predicament, Tenzer yelled out to Johnny and Jeanie, "You two; run for your lives and don't look back." He then motioned Johnny to catch his intelligent device, "I've connected to my brother; tell him to meet you at point 1023 Alpha-Omega. Now run!"

Johnny grabbed the device, gave a quick nod of thanks, and the two love birds ran with their hearts out.

Ronario and Miranda helped Tenzer immobilize all but one super-bike, the one that took the two out with one single volley of shots. Yana, as they had come to know, wasn't used to missing shots, and she had made it through their week defence, in search of the fleeing love birds.

"C'mon you bitch, show me what you got," Tenzer yelled at the top of his voice as he fired at will, not focussing on anything, but just hoping to distract Yana from her pursuit of the duo. But one shot from an officer positioned at the end behind him, tore open his back, as his mutilated body was flung in air and thrown meters away. Yana meanwhile had found the love birds, and this time she wasn't keen on getting them alive anymore.

"C'mon Tenzer, you can't fail me," Tenzer tried to talk some strength back to himself, as he realized the fate Johnny and Jeanie were facing were he to fail today.

His weapon had fallen a meter away from him, but half his body, including his one lung, had already been blown open. He had but only one arm and one leg to crawl with. The police women behind him had realized that every belligerent had been likely taken out, and were closing in fast.

"You can do it Tenzer," Tenzer said to himself, and he used his available arm and leg to give his body a couple of big heaves towards the weapon.

Yana meanwhile had flown around the running duo more than a few times, missing her shots only because she thought she could play a while. Little did she expect to run into trouble! But one shot from Tenzer, just as she had flown back and away from the border, and her super-bike was left useless. Lucky for Yana she landed safely on her feet, just as her companions finally took out Tenzer. But

with the bike lost, Yana was left to chase the love birds on foot, and the duo had already taken some lead over her.

"Run you bastards, run," a frustrated and enraged Yana quipped as she eased her pace just as the duo approached the border, "Where will you go from here?"

Yana was confident the force field won't let them across, but Tenzer had already done his job. Three 'Global Defence Force' manned crafts flew thick and fast out of the night sky from the US side, and reached the border just in time to stop Yana from making a kill, and eased the border field to let the love-birds cross over.

When the three planes landed, one on WFA side, and two on the US side, a young officer stepped out of one of them.

"This is Major Anthony Grahams," the officer informed a panting Johnny and Jeanie, "One of our colleagues stationed in YT Canada just reported in that we were needed here."

"Major Grahams, this is Detective Yana Ivanikova of the Alaskan Police Department, and these two here are fugitives of law," Yana however interrupted the conversation even before it had started, "I request the army transfers their custody to me and my colleagues immediately, so that appropriate legal proceedings may be instituted against the two."

"May I remind the officer that she is fifty miles outside her jurisdiction, well and truly in 'Global Defence Force' administered territory," the Major however reminded Yana the legal hurdle she wasn't in a position to surmount, "Whether these two here have committed a crime, or any legal proceedings should be instituted against them, shall be determined by the GDF authorities." He then turned to Johnny and Jeanie, and asked, "Which side of the border would you two like to face the army court?"

"The US side," both Johnny and Jeanie replied in unison.

Jeanie Johnny

"When reason marries fact, progress is born."

Chapter Fifteen: Love thee found

Dated: 2ⁿᵈ February, 2119

Emotions drag a person further and further away from the shore of logic, and towards the depths of illusion. Emotions are about doing what one knows is not the best thing to do, but which still ought to be done to satisfy ego; for a personal victory. Such victories however, are the culmination of selfish quests that seldom consider the greater good that could otherwise emerge out of deeds. Vengeance is sweet for the one avenged, but leaves the society bitter, for vengeance seeks more vengeance. Love of a beloved is a selfish pursuit that satisfies one heart, but could leave many others trampled. Of course, it is hard to argue that any of these deeds are avoidable, for else life itself might stop.

Of an order higher however, are deeds that have the potential to serve a larger purpose. When personal needs get tied up with a fundamental question that troubles a society at large, the selfish interests become social causes. But is one a torch-bearer for the society, or merely an arsonists, can only be determined by the application of reasoning to the situation. If the efforts yield a positive outcome, that adds value to social life, then the quest loses the selfish traits from its character. It then becomes a guiding light for others to look up to and follow. Protagonists become heroes, and situations become history!

Many such histories however, are written with quills drenched in blood; some innocent, some questionable, and some more blameworthy. But histories serve to protect much more in future, for they are the encyclopaedia of mistakes. They present the mistakes in their ugliest form, and also extrapolate the results that emerged out of them, giving future an opportunity to amend its' choices. Jeanie and Johnny's struggle for survival could be a guide post for many generations to come; to know where and how law could falter, what mistakes societies are prone to make, and what it really takes to challenge an established norm even when the norm is of dubious quality.

Jeanie and Johnny made a good choice; to cross over the border, for borders, in addition to territories, can also often divide cultural inconsistencies. As their story unfolded in front of the full bench of 'Global Defence Force' tribunal, what became abundantly clear was that the two would not have received a fair trial in the society staking claim to their custody. The fact that merely being in love with a person of the other sex was deemed enough to detain Johnny, and the fact that the threat of physical and sexual violence was real to both of them; was enough to convince the tribunal to rule there was a real threat of denial of basic human rights to the two.

The tribunal then considered the evidence that supported their arduous journey to escape, the brutal murder of their close friend Alena, their decision not to kill any of the 'Brazen Babes', their becoming live shooting targets of a maniac police officer, and their lack of options when finally accepting the assistance of 'Nature's Warriors Against Immorality' assets, who were acting on their own motion, and were in no way affiliated to the duo. The tribunal compared it with the desperate measure Jeanie had to take at the airport, that of deliberately hitting two robotic police personal, and came to the conclusion that it could be classified as self-defence. The tribunal eventually found the two innocent of any offences claimed against their name, and set them free with an option to return either to WFA and SFU, or seek asylum in the US. Johnny and Jeanie however knew what they had bargained for as their future, and hence opted for the latter option.

Barely five months after their escape, and living peacefully in a beautiful cottage by a riverside in Virginia, the two however, were unprepared for the surprise that knocked at their door this fateful day.

"Mom, dad," a shocked and surprise Johnny exclaimed as he opened the door to two familiar faces; Malvin and Sweena.

"How are you son," Malvin asked as the duo embraced each other like none would ever be able to separate them.

"Save some love for your mother, won't you," Sweena chided as Johnny finally emerged from his embrace with his father, to embrace his mother.

"And what about us," asked Josha, as he walked towards the door with Juliandra by his side.

"Mom, dad," a delighted Jeanie rushed out, having been intrigued by the sounds of jubilation coming from the front door. And she rushed straight into Josha's arms, and Juliandra joined the duo in embrace.

It was a shocking surprise for both, and in more ways than one, for the way their parents had arrived, was intriguing on its own.

"What have we missed," Johnny finally asked when everybody had settled down in the living room.

"Well, as it happened," Malvin started the reply, "Your flight put us together in one house for the first time. While I am sure your experience was as much physically

challenging as much it was emotionally draining, unlike you, we were not emotionally charged. Rather, we were all breaking down; worried about you, worried about what would happen."

"And then your tribunal case started," Josha added, "Leaving us suspended in the middle of the storm of uncertainty."

"As time flew by, days became weeks," Malvin continued, "Soon enough, we started to realize, all the time that we had spent over the years chatting behind your backs; we had actually grown very fond of each other. We, I and Sweena, and Josha and Juliandra, knew much more about each other as mixed couples, than we had known about each other as married couples."

"The day your verdict came out, and Malvin and Josha finally left us," Juliandra continued from where Malvin left, "Was the first day we all realized; we actually can't live without each other. In fact, we realized we should have always lived together."

"And would you believe," Josha quipped nodding his head, "We found love again in our lives. Or should I say; we discovered that we had always already been in love with those that we had never thought about like that."

"What!" exclaimed a surprised Jeanie.

"Wait, are you saying," Johnny however was perplexed, but he didn't need to finish his question to get an answer.

"Yes son," Malvin replied, "I am marrying Sweena, and Josha is marrying Juliandra. Now will you help us find two nice homes somewhere in your neighbourhood."

"No way," a shocked and delighted Johnny jumped out of his couch, "This is just amazing." He then looked at Jeanie, whose eyes had already filled up.

Jeanie finally broke down, and started to sob, with her face held between her palms.

"Hey, my Sweet-pie-overload," Johnny knelt down on the couch by her side, and took her in his arms, "It's alright! We are finally a big family now."

And the two slowly stood up, and then embraced each other hard. This time their kiss was soft, but full of love; blissful.

The two new couples on the block, they looked at them with adulation, and then at each other in satisfaction. Their families had been reunited and reborn at the same time.

About the Author

'Fatal Urge Carefree Kiss' is the artistic alias of 'Amanpreet Singh Rai'; a Forensic Expert (M.Sc), a teacher (B.Ed), and a Lawyer (LLB) by education, and a writer and producer by choice and training.

Starting out in 2010 with two concurrent novel series; 'God of a man' and 'Mishiida Alexander', Aman has so far penned eight completed literary works, including 'Jeanie Johnny'. In addition, he has written a movie script; 'Incidentals – The Brides' grooms', a project currently open for investment partnerships.

While the two novel series; 'God of a man' and 'Mishiida Alexander', set in two universes parallel to ours; have only been available as e-books so far, 'Jeanie Johnny' is his first work to be published in hard copy. Another novel series, 'The White Warrior', was pushed back to accommodate 'Jeanie Johnny', This third series is expected to be a three book story, set in Tolkien Universe post Tolkien times.

As a producer, Aman is currently working on his fourth English album, and first Punjabi album. With his Punjabi album he is set to launch his brother as a singer. He has so far produced three music videos, all based on concepts developed by him, and the last two directed by him as well.